# WHEN WILL THE
# SECRETS END?

A MARGE CHRISTENSEN MYSTERY

# WHEN WILL THE
# SECRETS END?

## PATRICIA K. BATTA

LILLIMAR PUBLISHING
PRESCOTT, ARIZONA

PUBLISHED BY LILLIMAR PUBLISHING

www.lillimarpublishing.com


Cataloguing-in-Publication Data

Batta, Patricia K.
    When will the secrets end? : a Marge Christensen mystery / Patricia K. Batta.
    — Prescott, Arizona : Lillimar Publishing, [2015]
        pages ; cm
    ISBN: 978-0-9966843-0-9 (paperback)
    ISBN: 978-0-9966843-1-6 (e-book)

    1. Christensen, Marge (Fictitious character) 2. Foster children—Fiction. 3. Older child adoption—Fiction.  4. Custody of children— Fiction.  5. Grandfathers— Fiction.  6. Women drug addicts—Fiction.  7. Bellevue (Wash.)—Fiction. 8. Pasco (Wash.)—Fiction. 9. Washington (State)—Fiction. 10. Mystery fiction. I. Title.

    PS3602.A898 W446 2016        2015948587
    813/.6—dc23                  1510

This is a work of fiction. Names, characters, places, events, and incidents are either the product of the author's imagination or are used fictitiously. The author's use of places or businesses is not intended to change the entirely fictional character of the work. In all other respects, any resemblance to persons living or dead, businesses, companies, events, or locales is entirely coincidental.

Cover and text design by Mary Jo Zazueta
www.tothepointsolutions.com


Printed in the United States of America
First Edition

# WHEN WILL THE
# SECRETS END?

# ONE

~~~~~~~~~

"Why do I have to see that old man? He never did nothin' for me."

Marge steered her aging Honda wagon around another sharp mountain curve before glancing at the surly twelve-year-old sitting beside her. He was paying no attention to the fresh vista of snow-capped mountains.

"He's your grandfather," she said. "He wants to meet you." She struggled to maintain a calm face to prevent Eric from sensing her own apprehension. What had started as a slight pain behind her left ear began to throb as it crept across the back of her head. Was she doing the right thing by insisting he meet his grandfather?

Eric snorted, hunched his narrow shoulders, and stared out the window, refusing to meet Marge's eye. "So where was he all this time?"

Good question, Marge thought. Alfred Landon, Eric's paternal grandfather, lived in a rural area near Pasco, Washington, a little over three hours from Bellevue. Not a great enough distance to explain why Eric had never met him.

Child Protective Services always kept Landon informed about his grandson. They let him know when Eric ran away from home to escape his father's abuse. They let him know when his grandson was placed in foster care. Twice CPS returned Eric home because his father appeared to have his drinking under control—it didn't last for long.

CPS contacted Landon again when Eric's father finally lost his parental rights because he continued to beat Eric. Still Landon didn't respond—not until he was notified that Pete and Marge wanted to adopt Eric. Then Alfred Landon decided to meet his grandson. Why?

"You don't have to do this," Olivia, Eric's caseworker and Marge's soon-to-be daughter-in-law told her. "I'm not even sure CPS will give you permission to take Eric out of King County. If Landon wants to see his grandson, he needs to make arrangements with CPS; they will probably require he come to Bellevue. I doubt he'll do that. He's shown no interest until now."

Nevertheless, Marge had insisted. They couldn't wait for CPS to put the wheels in motion and then wait to see if Landon would take advantage of the opportunity. Marge and Pete wanted to start adoption proceedings, and they needed to be sure nothing would come back to bite them after they raised Eric's hopes. Olivia was in full agreement with that. The boy had already gone through enough hurt and disappointment in his twelve years. Marge wasn't quite sure how she did it, but Olivia got permission for Marge to make the drive with Eric.

Skirting the edge of Keechelus Lake after crossing Snoqualmie Pass, Marge glanced again at the thin, tense figure beside her. Neither the rugged peaks surrounding them nor the rock-blasting sites that marred the landscape as they neared the summit caught his attention. He didn't even glance at this large lake on a plateau, so vast it felt as if they were in the middle of a prairie, not near the top of a mountain range.

They would have to take this trip another time, she thought. When Eric's hazel eyes weren't dull with the curtain he used to hide his fear. When he could enjoy the majesty of the mountains and the vibrant greens of the forest. When they could stop at Snoqualmie Falls before crossing the summit, and gorge themselves on crab legs in Ellensburg or picnic in Snoqualmie State Park. When Eric had learned to believe life could be good.

"Want to stop for lunch?" she asked, breaking the long silence. "It's a little early, but I don't know if we'll find a good place to eat between Ellensburg and Pasco." The mention of food usually grabbed Eric's attention. In addition to a normal twelve-year-old's appetite, he dealt with the memory of many hungry nights out on the streets where he stayed to escape his father's drunken rampages.

Eric shrugged. His expression remained blank.

"Well, I need to stretch. I think we'll stop in Ellensburg before we switch from I-90 to I-82. After that it'll be a straight shot to the tri-cities area and to your grandfather's."

Marge detected a slight shudder at her mention of his grandfather. She had to admit to a shiver of anxiety herself as she wondered what lay ahead for them.

Pre-teen boys, especially those who had experienced real hunger in their lives, do not let much interfere with the demands of their stomachs. Eric was no exception. While Marge nibbled on a salad at the Roadhouse Cafe, he managed to put away a double burger, fries, and a milkshake, all without looking up or cracking a smile. One would never guess he'd demolished breakfast a little over two hours ago. The sight of his sandy-brown head bent over his food brought Marge close to tears, almost overwhelmed by a stab of affection.

Eric had bonded more with her husband, Pete. Eric was the tough guy, the one who had been protector and champion to their other foster child, Benjamin, during the boys' years on the streets and moving in and out of several foster-care situations, some good, some bad, before they moved in with Pete and Marge. Benjamin had been the first to tug at Marge's heartstrings, because his need for acceptance was clear. Eric, being the older one, hid behind his tough-guy stance. It was rare for Marge and Eric to be alone together. She could only hope one result of this trip would be a closer relationship between them.

Marge put her cup down. She tried to rub away the tension and continuing pain at the back of her neck as she thought about the phone call she received from Olivia early this morning. She had nearly put the trip on hold.

"Benjamin's mother is out of rehab," Olivia had told her. "I haven't been able to find out yet if she was released early for some reason or if she simply managed to walk away on her own. Once Benjamin knows she's out, you know he is going to try to find her."

It could only have been a few hours since Benjamin's mother left rehab. She was probably sober and drug-free for the moment. She wouldn't be for long. Unfortunately, Benjamin never gave up hope. As soon as he knew his mother was out, Marge was sure he would busy himself trying to figure out how to protect her from the life she had fallen into. Even if the system finally admitted Benjamin's mother would never be able to take care of him and permanently severed parental rights, he was unlikely to agree to the final separation adoption would mean.

"What would happen if we didn't tell him?" she had asked Pete before leaving home.

He shook his head. "He'll most likely find out some-how. If he thinks we won't always be straight with him, we will lose his trust. As much as we want to shield Ben from the results of his mother's actions, we can never keep the truth from him."

Marge had hesitated, indecision gnawing at her. "Maybe I should put off the trip to Pasco. Benjamin will need me."

Pete shook his head. "I wasn't sure you should go, but you need to get Eric away from here before he finds out about Ben's mother or they'll both be out on the streets looking for her. And Eric is a lot more resourceful about how to stay hidden than Ben is."

So, even though she decided to make the trip, Marge and Eric got a late start and it was already close to noon. Marge ran a hand through her riot of auburn curls as she watched Eric slurp the last of his milkshake. She tried hard not to judge. She knew alcohol and drug addictions were illnesses some people could not overcome. It was difficult for Marge to excuse, though. How could a mother not respond to a child's pain?

When Eric had finished eating, Marge tossed the remnants of her salad and squared her shoulders. It was dif-ficult, but necessary, to leave Benjamin in Pete and Olivia's capable hands. She and Eric had to go to Pasco to meet Eric's grandfather. Clearing the air with the man was the only way they could end the suspense about what he might do to disrupt their lives. They would return to Bellevue tomorrow, hopefully with Eric's situation settled, so they could then deal with Benjamin's.

# TWO

~~~~~~~~~~

Marge could hardly believe her computer-generated directions to Alfred Landon's home took them over roads that deteriorated from paved to gravel to dirt—all the way to what looked like a long and rutted driveway. How did someone learn about all these back roads in order to put them on a national mapping system and provide step-by-step instructions?

Marge turned in and peered ahead, fearing for the frame of her old car as she crept up the driveway. A moment later, just as the house came into view, she slammed on the brakes. The apparition weaving unsteadily in the middle of the lane in front of them could only be Eric's grandfather. He carried a shotgun in his hand.

Marge turned to Eric. His face was pale, his eyes wide. The pained look in them told her he had seen the same thing. The man was an older, even more wasted version of Eric's father; in fact, a terribly damaged version of Eric himself. One glance at his bleary eyes and shaky hands told Marge no one would consider him a suitable person to take custody of a child.

Marge frowned. Why was Alfred Landon walking down the driveway toward them? He didn't appear to be in any condition to walk at all. Did he think whatever was inside the house would hurt his chances of gaining custody of Eric more than his inebriation?

The exterior of the house did not bode well for what might be inside. Marge took in the peeling, dirty, white paint; missing shingles on the roof; and a couple of boarded windows surrounded by a scruffy yard that seemed to be more sand than reedy grass. All of which contrasted with the lush, irrigated fields of grapevines surrounding the homestead.

Like the house, Alfred Landon appeared used up. With sallow skin and yellow teeth, his hazel eyes were a pale replica of his grandson's. A slight breeze carried the scent of whiskey through the open car window. He listed to the side, as if finding it difficult to stand against the breeze.

"Stay here," Marge said, stepping out and around to the front of the car to face Alfred. Eric ignored her instruction and appeared at her side a few seconds later. No surprise there.

Alfred stopped and cradled the shotgun in his arms before declaring, "He's my blood. You got no right to him."

Marge squeezed Eric's shoulder until he winced before she realized she was hurting him. Why had she come here first? There would be no reasoning with this man. Why hadn't she alerted local law enforcement about what she was doing?

"I do have legal custody of him." Marge struggled to speak up, to not allow fear to show in her voice. "We came here today to find out why you have taken a sudden interest in Eric after all these years."

"Cuz he's my blood. If his pa can't handle him, I can." Landon took a step toward them and glowered at Eric.

Marge stepped back. This didn't make any sense. Alfred couldn't possibly believe he could get custody of Eric this way. She shook her head. Did she really expect a person as drunk as Alfred to make any sense?

Alfred took another step and moved the shotgun from its cradled position into his hands. Marge stumbled back, taking Eric with her. Would he really shoot at her? Was he too drunk to realize he might hit Eric instead? She slipped her left hand into the pocket where she kept her cell phone.

"We're going to leave now, Mr. Landon," she said, trying to keep her voice calm. "I'd like to talk with you about Eric, but we can't do it this way. If you have any interest in seeing him, arrange to meet me in town tomorrow morning."

"Boy, why don't you come over here where you belong?"

Landon made another move toward them, reaching out as if to grab Eric's arm and nearly falling forward in the process. Eric balled his fists, tensing into a fighting stance. Marge pushed him behind her.

"Eric, get in the car right now," she commanded, surprised at the authority she heard in her voice. To her relief, after a slight hesitation, he did what he was told. Marge pulled her cell phone out as she stepped carefully backward toward the car, never taking her eyes off his grandfather.

She dialed 911 by feel, making sure Landon could see what she was doing. Glancing at the phone, she realized she didn't have a signal. Would Landon know the call hadn't gone through?

"I am being threatened with a shotgun at Alfred Landon's place on Touchstone Lane," she said loudly, hoping to fool him. She couldn't calm her thoughts enough to remember the address and didn't dare look away from Landon to find it. "Do you know where that is?" She skirted around to the driver's side of the car. The old man stopped and cocked his head, as if measuring her words.

Once she reached the door, she grabbed it open and jumped in the car, throwing the cell phone toward Eric. She hit the door lock and jammed the key into the ignition. Shifting into reverse, she trod on the gas pedal. The wheels spun as the car started moving. Glancing back at Landon, she gasped. He had raised the shotgun to his shoulder. The way it weaved back and forth, who knew where the shot might end up? Could he actually hit anything near what he tried to aim at?

She slammed on the brakes, shifted into drive, gears grinding, and hit the gas pedal again. The car shot forward. Landon's eyes widened, his shotgun wavering. Marge stopped breathing and braked hard, praying she wouldn't hit him. Her breath came out in a small explosion when he jumped aside, falling to the ground, and the gun skittered away. Shifting again, Marge gunned the motor and sped back, stomping on the brakes to keep from running off the other side of the road. A cloud of dust billowed up behind them as she raced down the dirt road, back toward the small town they had passed through on their way there.

It was a few minutes before Marge could breathe normally enough to speak. "Are you all right?" she asked.

"Yeah," Eric said, exhaling a pent-up breath. "Where'd you learn to drive like that?"

Marge looked over to see his eyes staring at her, wide with wonder.

She bit back the wave of near hysteria triggered by relief. At least Eric wasn't traumatized by his grandfather's actions. Why would he be? He had suffered far worse living with his father.

"Not bad for an old lady, huh?" she said, struggling to hold back laughter.

"So, can we go home now?" Eric asked.

"Not just yet," Marge said, sobered by the question. "We need to check with the local authorities to see if your grandfather has done anything bad enough to prevent any possibility of him getting custody of you. Olivia said CPS couldn't find a record, but not having a record doesn't mean he hasn't done something here that we can use against him if we need to."

"Don't call him my grandfather. I don't want nothin' to do with that old man. And I'll never go live with him—ever."

"I understand. But if we can prove upfront he isn't a suitable guardian for you, we won't have to fight about it later."

Even as Marge spoke, she realized she was treading on shaky ground. She was assuring Eric of something she couldn't guarantee. What would happen to him, and his trust of people, if she couldn't follow through?

# THREE

Alfred Landon lived in an out-of-the-way spot in agricultural Franklin County. While doing some research to help Eric learn about the origins of his family, Marge had discovered the area was home to several national food-processing plants. While apples were the main crop, along with cherries and hops, the number of vineyards and wineries continued to expand.

A sign informed them they were entering Dusty Township; soon they saw a scattering of buildings. Marge looked around as she drove through the small town. One side of the street appeared to be the township center, consisting of a police station with the township offices and fire station on one side of it and a library on the other. All three buildings were a uniform shade of tan that blended with their surroundings.

On the other side of the street were a combination general store and hardware with a post office sign in the window; a small gas station; a diner with neon lights spelling out The Dusty Café; and a hair salon/barbershop. Construction was in progress on two more buildings. Signs promised they would soon be home to an auto repair shop and a grocery store. Something was revitalizing Dusty. It looked like a ghost town getting a facelift.

Marge parallel parked on the quiet street, and she and Eric headed to the police station, which seemed remarkably sturdy for a building styled like those built in the coal mining days. Either the building had been extensively overhauled or a new building had been built to mimic that era.

A man on his way out held the door open for them. Marge looked up to give him a smile of thanks but he appeared to be too deep in thought to notice. The room inside was freshly painted and orderly.

Another man, who Marge assumed was a deputy, looked up from his desk, took one look at Eric, and called out, "Hey, Carl! You got another brother here."

A man sauntered in from a back room. Marge's eyes popped open, understanding what the deputy meant. Eric could be this man in about twenty years. The same hazel eyes and sandy brown hair, the same lean and wiry build. Marge frowned. For some reason she had thought Eric's father, Jerry, was Alfred's only child.

He studied Marge as he approached. "Don't tell me the old man suckered a looker like you," he said.

"What? Of course not." Marge felt her face grow hot.

"Glad to hear it. So, where did this young whelp come from?"

"His father lost custody of him. My husband and I want to adopt Eric, but his grandfather is making waves; so we came from Bellevue to see if we can straighten things out."

Carl snorted. "There's nothing straight about old Al. Why did Jerry lose custody?"

Marge hesitated. She wasn't sure it was good for Eric to hear them discuss his relationship with his father, but she knew she'd never convince him to leave. "Jerry is an alcoholic. He becomes violent when he drinks. He beat Eric one too many times after promising to reform so CPS terminated his parental rights."

Carl's face clouded. "Poor sod."

Marge realized he was not talking about Eric.

"Jerry had to live with the brute," Carl continued. "You can't grow up with abuse and not get tainted."

"I am confused. How are you related? You can't be Eric's brother. Are you Jerry's?"

"I presume I'm this young man's uncle. His half-uncle, I guess you'd say. His grandfather seduced or raped my mother; we've never been sure which because she wouldn't talk about it. Anyway, I'm the result. My mother committed suicide when I was a year old. My mother's parents said she did it because she was traumatized by Alfred stalking her, but they couldn't prove anything. My grandparents kept me and raised me as their own."

Marge's head reeled at the spate of information. "Why couldn't CPS find a record of any of this?" she asked. She could only surmise Carl was so open about his parentage because it explained his relationship to Eric, but she wished he had not burdened the boy with quite so much knowledge about his grandfather.

"My grandparents never did anything to make the arrangement legal. My mother and I had already been living with them, so nobody thought anything of it. They told me Alfred never showed any interest in either of us. Everyone knew I belonged to my grandparents."

"What about Jerry's mother? Was she Alfred's wife?"

"She was, poor soul. A fire broke out and destroyed a small building on their land where she spent a lot of time.

Again, no one knows whether it was an accident or suicide or murder. There was no evidence to pin it on Alfred. He claimed she liked to go there for some peace and quiet, and sometimes used candles or burned incense in the place. Maybe Jerry could tell you more, but he was pretty young at the time. After his wife's death, I guess Alfred started drinking. I don't know how or when he connected with my mother. The why might be easier to figure out if you take a good look at both of them. No one would ever talk to me about it."

Marge looked at Carl. "The deputy said 'you've got another brother.' How many of you are there?"

Carl shrugged. "We don't know for sure. Alfred was a charmer, and good looking, until he got lost in the bottle." Carl's face reddened as if he realized saying Alfred was handsome was like praising himself. "Over the next few years, a couple of married women in the area became pregnant and the timing made their husbands suspicious; and a couple of teenage girls did, too. None of the women talked. Townspeople liked to blame Alfred, but without someone's testimony there wasn't a shred of evidence."

Marge shook her head. It was hard to square the wasted drunk she had seen at Alfred Landon's place with the town's irresistible bad boy. "So, where are all of these people now? Have any of them contacted Alfred?"

"One of the teenagers left town with her parents. Knowing the family, she probably had the baby, but we don't know anything for sure. The other one was sent away, too. The gossip mill says her parents made her have an abortion before they shuffled her off to boarding school. The parents also left town soon after.

"One of the husbands divorced his wife and she moved to Walla Walla. That was her son, Dan, leaving as you came in. His mother's ex-husband recently died, and she finally admitted the man wasn't Dan's biological father. Dan was here looking for directions to Alfred's house. I didn't ask why. I assume it was because he had somehow found out Alfred was his father.

"The other husband stuck with his wife and they moved to Pasco shortly after Leroy was born. I don't think Leroy's mother ever admitted to anything, but you know how things get around in small towns. Neither of them looks like Alfred—not like Jerry and I do—and now Eric, too. I guess these days they could do DNA testing, but no one wants to prove a relationship to Alfred Landon, so it will probably never be done."

"I got bad blood," Eric said, his voice small.

Marge swallowed a surge of guilt, her head still whirling as she tried to take it all in. The conversation had definitely gone further than what he needed to hear.

"Eric," she said, "take a good look at Carl. He obviously has many of the same genes you do, and he appears to have grown into a fine young man. Your father is the way he is because of what he had to deal with while he was growing up. From everything I know about you, I think we've rescued you in time."

Carl squatted down to Eric's level, sitting back on one heel. "Your father was already in deep trouble by the time he was your age. The only reason he didn't go to juvenile detention was because back in those days, especially in this town, people tried to bury their problems rather than deal with them. If he had gone into foster care, like you did,

15

away from his father, he might have been able to have a good life.

"I understand how you feel, though. I felt the same way for a long time. I was afraid to have children. First, I was afraid alcoholism might be genetic. And even if it wasn't, could I have bursts of temper and hurt my children the way Alfred did your dad? But I am married now and have a son and a daughter, and we have a great life. I know you can do the same."

Marge felt tears of gratitude well up in her eyes. This trip had been worth it, if only to have Carl say those words to Eric.

"Since there is no documentation in the court system of Alfred Landon's alcoholism or mistreatment of Jerry, it is possible he could have a claim to Eric as his next closest relative," she said. Eric tensed again beside her.

Carl stood and looked down at them from his six-foot height. "Alfred Landon gets into some kind of trouble every time he turns around. We mostly ignore him; he's like part of the landscape. We don't have to ignore him. He could do something for which we would arrest him at any time; he might even find himself facing serious jail time. If he is reminded of all the possible consequences of his actions, he may decide he's better off the way things are.

"Besides, I'm sure we have enough people to testify to Alfred's unsuitability. I can't imagine he would ever be granted custody. If I'm wrong and none of that works, he may have to get what he deserves, because I'm not going to let him ruin another life."

Carl reached out his right hand to Eric and waited for Eric to put out his own. With a firm handshake, he said, "That is a promise, young man."

# FOUR

~~~~~~~~~~

Because there was no motel in Dusty, Marge had reserved a room in Pasco before leaving Bellevue. She hadn't printed out directions to the motel because she didn't know where she would be, so she didn't have a starting point. She asked Carl if he could download a map on the office computer.

"No need. I live in Pasco right now, though we'll be moving back with my parents here in Dusty next month," he said. "I'm ready to head home. Why don't you follow me? We can stop at Pizza Hut for a bite to eat and get better acquainted. By then it will be late enough for you to check in at the motel."

Eric devoured one slice of pizza and started shredding a second one, a frown on his face. Marge and Carl exchanged a look, but waited him out.

"Did my dad's father really beat him, too?" he finally asked. "Do you think he beats me because his dad beat him?"

"Yes, people say your grandfather beat your father when he was drinking. Most of what you might want to know about happened before I was old enough to understand it. And my grandparents didn't want me involved with your father at all. So, what I know is from the gossip mill, same as everyone else in town, and not to be trusted as actual fact."

Eric fidgeted some more. Finally, he looked up and asked in a tiny voice, "Did you know my mother?"

"No, I'm sorry, I didn't. Your parents were a little older than me, and they moved to Seattle." He stopped, eyes narrowed in thought. "I just realized I don't know if they got married before or after they moved to Seattle." His frown deepened. "Or if they ever married at all."

Marge berated herself for not having considered Eric's natural desire to learn about his mother. It would be especially good if she had known about his parents' marital status before Carl blindsided them with the possibility they weren't married. Marge knew nothing about her, or how old Eric was when she died. She and Pete had been too busy integrating the boys into their lives to spend much time investigating their pasts.

She shook her head. She would have to find out what she could, but they had enough on their plates right now. They might have to wait until they got back to Bellevue to begin researching Eric's mother.

~

Carl carried their bags to the lobby of the motel and waited while Marge checked in. Eric's face turned red and he shuffled his feet.

"What's the matter?" Marge asked.

"We're ... uh ... sleeping in the same room?" he asked.

Marge stopped and stared at him. "I hadn't planned on paying for two rooms," she managed to say, but Eric's question raised an issue she hadn't thought about. If this were a twelve-year-old Robert, she wouldn't hesitate. Robert was her son. If Eric was to be her son, there should be no problem with him, either. It wasn't that simple, of course. They didn't have a history of being mother and son together.

Many would consider Eric too old to sleep in the same room with an unrelated woman, maybe even with his own mother. Perhaps this was a way to start building a history, but not if it raised questions about her suitability as a parent. She hesitated to leave Eric in a room by himself, but quickly realized how silly she was being. The boy had been on his own out in the streets of Bellevue and Seattle much of his life. She was sure he could handle being in a motel room by himself. Especially if they could get connecting rooms.

She turned back to the counter to see if it could be arranged.

"You don't need to get two rooms," Carl said, as if reading her thoughts. "If you trust Eric to me, he can stay at my house and get to know his cousins. I know they would like to meet him. How about you, Eric?"

Marge could see the struggle going on behind Eric's eyes. He didn't trust easily. Still, he must be curious about this newfound family. He finally gave a half nod to Carl, who looked at Marge for permission.

Marge hesitated only a moment. She wasn't quite sure

why, but she trusted Carl. And, after all, he was almost family. "Yes, I think it would be good for Eric and avoid an awkward situation here." The look in Carl's eyes told her he understood her concern. "Are you sure it will be all right with your wife, though?"

Carl grinned. "My wonderful wife will be delighted."

"How are we going to get in touch with Alfred Landon tomorrow to see if he plans to come in and talk?" Marge asked.

"He doesn't have a telephone. I'll drive out first thing in the morning to find out what he has in mind. Why don't you come to my house for breakfast?"

"If it isn't an imposition on your wife, I'll take you up on the offer."

"No imposition. Angela loves company and she loves Seattle. You'll probably have to answer a hundred questions about what is going on in the big city."

Marge laughed, wondering how many answers she would have since she rarely left suburban Bellevue to brave the traffic in Seattle.

Carl wrote down his phone number and the directions to his house and left with Eric. Marge hoped the decision to spend time apart didn't interfere with her plans for bonding on this trip, because in her mind and in her heart Eric was already her son. Returning to the front desk to correct the reservation, she decided it might be wise to reserve her room for a second night. She thought everything could be cleared up tomorrow, but there was always the chance it wouldn't. With any luck, she would be able to cancel the reservation and head home.

Marge rinsed her face with cold water and stared into

the mirror before settling into her room. Her normally startling green eyes were dull with fatigue and worry. She felt
more alone than she could remember ever feeling before.
Yet, she had lived alone several years before marrying Pete.
Her life had become so full in the last year; first, being
married to a larger-than-life man who filled her world
completely; second, agreeing to take on Eric and Benjamin
before she and Pete even had their honeymoon. She picked
up the phone and dialed their home number.

Marge relaxed at the sound of Pete's voice. She outlined
what had happened and described Eric's extended family
in the area. "So, according to Carl, Alfred's reputation is so
bad we have nothing to worry about. Still, I'd like to come
to some kind of understanding and feel more secure before
leaving."

"You do whatever you need to do," Pete said. "I trust
your instincts for handling the situation."

"May I talk to Benjamin?"

The line was silent for a moment. "He's not home yet."

Marge's breath caught. "It's kind of late, isn't it?"

"Not really. You must be tired from the drive to think it
is. Anyway, I'm going to give him some leeway. He said he
was going out with friends. If he isn't home by nine, I'll try
to track him down."

"What friends? I didn't know he had any friends in our
neighborhood yet. Are you sure he doesn't know where his
mother is?"

Pete sighed. "The boys started meeting other kids as
soon as we moved in, Marge. Kids seem to be able to make
friends faster than adults. When we had dinner it didn't
appear he had heard his mother is out. He did seem a little

moody, which could be a result of missing you and Eric. He took off after dinner and I hoped going out with friends would help him work off some tension, whatever is causing it."

"I'll wind things up here as quickly as possible and hope to be home tomorrow afternoon."

Marge disconnected and frowned. It was difficult being so far away at a time like this. Benjamin might need her. His mother, who he did his best to protect, had been in rehab several times for her drug use. An eleven-year-old might not realize rehab was the best place for her, and she knew Ben would try to help her stay out. She shook her head. Nothing she could do right now would help Benjamin. Once she completed what she came here to do she could go home and concentrate on his needs. If all went well, she would be home tomorrow afternoon.

Marge pulled her sketchpad out of her suitcase and began to draw—something she often did to calm her mind and get her thoughts straight. On the first blank page she sketched Alfred Landon, Carl, and Eric. They were eerily similar. If she added Jerry's face, she knew it would be similar, too. On the next page, she sketched the face of Dan, the man who had opened the door for them at the Dusty police station, who Carl said might also be Alfred's son. She couldn't see any resemblance.

Marge remembered that, according to Carl, Dan's mother had told him her ex-husband was not Dan's biological dad. What had she told him about Alfred Landon?

Marge lay back on the bed and closed her eyes. It was good Pete trusted her instincts. That made one of them.

# FIVE

~~~~~~~~

Pete pulled his hand down over his face after he disconnected. Today his department had wrapped up a major homicide investigation that had kept him out early and late for over a week. He badly needed to crash and get a good night's sleep. He couldn't do that until Ben came home though.

He had not exactly lied to Marge—he wouldn't do that—but he was not as relaxed about Ben being out as he had pretended. Ben had raced out before Pete could talk to him; so Pete decided to wait and see what happened. They had always been somewhat lenient about curfew for Eric and Ben anyway, because the boys had been accustomed to living on the streets and it would be easy to drive them back out there by being too strict.

Ben was pushing it tonight. Pete would have to be careful how he handled the situation. As tired as he was, it would be easy to lash out.

He was glad he hadn't made a big deal of Ben's lateness to Marge. A lot of discussion had gone into whether she should drive across the mountains to erase any threats to their adopting Eric. Pete had finally agreed to her going, but if she was too worried about Ben, she would have a hard time concentrating on that task.

He answered the ring of his cell phone quickly, half expecting it to be Marge calling back.

"Pete, is Benjamin with you?"

It wasn't Marge. It was Olivia, Eric and Ben's caseworker and Robert's fiancée.

"No, he's out with friends. I'm beginning to worry about how late he is, though. Why?"

"Well, since his mother's staying in rehab was a requirement to keep her from being charged with prostitution, she will try to go underground—because I found out for sure she was not released. If she goes underground, I'm afraid she might take Benjamin with her."

Pete knew that. He had thought cutting Ben a little slack tonight was the right thing to do. Was he taking the risk too lightly? "Do you think Ben could have heard about his mother?" he asked. A rush of adrenaline pushed him to his feet, ready to head out and start looking. The back door opened.

Pete whirled around. Ben stood just inside the door, muscles tense, blue eyes wary. Pete tried to keep from reacting. It wouldn't take much to make the boy bolt back out into the night.

Turning away to keep Ben from hearing, Pete said, "He just walked in. I'll try to find out what he knows and where he has been." Pete ended the phone call and turned back to Ben. "You are a little late tonight," he said, trying to keep any hint of disapproval out of his voice.

"Yeah," was all Ben said, not moving.

"I was just talking with Olivia. She told me your mother left rehab."

"Yeah," Ben repeated, tensing even more. He looked

ready to run. Pete was glad he had been open with Ben about his mother since he had obviously already found out.

This was going to be difficult. While Ben had come a long way in learning to trust Pete and Marge since they took him in, Pete being in law enforcement tended to keep the boy at arm's length. It truly was one of those times when he needed Marge. She had already raised two children and would have a better idea about how to handle the situation. Also, Ben had been drawn to Marge and her art talent from the beginning, making Ben more likely to listen to her. Somehow, Pete would have to bridge the gap by himself.

"Anything I can do to help?" he asked.

Ben eyed him with suspicion for a moment before his shoulders slumped. "I don't know where she is," he mumbled. "I got to look for her."

"Not tonight, son," Pete said, hoping he could make it stick. "Tomorrow we'll both look and other people will, too." Pete knew he couldn't commandeer the police force for a full-out search for a drug addict who voluntarily walked away from rehab, but at least they could keep their eyes open.

There was no trust in Ben's tear-filled eyes. "Yeah, so you can lock her up again."

Pete gently took Ben by the shoulder and led him to a chair at the dining table. Taking a seat across from him, Pete leaned forward. "Ben, you know your mother's drug addiction is a sickness. She needs help to get better. Rehab is like going to a hospital to get well. The only problem is that people with addictions crave what they are addicted to, so they fight the cure. The best way to help your mother is to keep her in the hospital until she stops fighting it."

"It'll kill her," Ben whispered hoarsely. "She can't stand to be locked up."

"It won't kill her, Ben. It only feels as if it will for a while, before it gets better."

"You don't know that. You don't understand her." Ben pushed his chair back from the table and rushed off to his room.

Pete sat back, heaving a sigh. At least Ben hadn't left the house. But Pete had no idea how he was going to keep the boy from going back out to find his mother. And if Ben found her, what would he decide he needed to do?

# SIX

On Tuesday morning Marge pulled into the driveway of a neat, one-story house with gray siding and white shutters. Someone had taken care to keep the small front lawn looking like a plush, green carpet; not an easy task in this desert-like environment. Even without the tall, weathered fence blocking the backyard from view, she would have known Carl's two children spent most of their outdoor time there.

Marge climbed the two steps to the entry. The door opened before she could knock. Nearly falling back down the steps, Marge heard herself gasp. With long, jet-black hair pulled into a loose ponytail and soft, brown eyes highlighting a smooth, olive complexion, this was possibly the most naturally beautiful woman Marge had ever seen. Marge's face grew warm in embarrassment, which she knew meant it had turned red.

"Welcome," the woman said, seeming unfazed by Marge's reaction. "I'm Angela, Carl's wife. Come on in and join us for breakfast." With graceful steps she led the way past a living room containing the practical furnishings of a home with children in it, where the only clutter was child-created, to the kitchen. Eric and a younger boy and girl sat at the breakfast bar, their plates stacked with pancakes swimming in maple syrup.

"Uh-oh. Looks like some people helped themselves to more syrup while I was answering the door."

Marge was pleased to see Eric duck his chin, a slight grin on his face. A short time ago he would have gone immediately into defense mode if caught doing something he might be chastised for. The other two children laughed out loud. Marge smiled at their mischievous faces but her heart constricted. What different lives Eric and Benjamin had lived. All children deserved to have the kind of carefree confidence these two displayed.

"This is Joey and Carla," Angela said. "Say good morning to Mrs. Peterson."

Neither child had inherited their father's strong resemblance to Alfred Landon. Carla had the good fortune to look like her mother. Joey, with dark hair and hazel eyes, was a striking combination of the two.

"What time did Carl leave?" Marge asked after she was seated at the breakfast bar with her own plate of pancakes.

"He left early, about an hour and a half ago. He was hoping to get there before Alfred had a chance to get drunk. However, one can't count on Alfred being sober any time of day, so it's hard to tell how long he will be."

The front door burst open and Carl charged in.

Marge was about to ask him how the meeting had gone, but the look on his face stopped her. With a warning glance at the children, he beckoned Marge and Angela into the living room.

"You remember I told you about Dan, the young man who came to see me, who said he had to talk to Alfred?"

"Yes."

"He's been murdered. I got the news before I arrived

at the scene. The county guys have taken over now; so I decided to detour back here to tell you in person before going to the office to take care of the paperwork."

"Why would you need to tell me in person?" Marge asked.

Carl looked at her. "Because it happened at Alfred Landon's place. The victim was evidently shot in the face point blank with a shotgun. Alfred's shotgun was found at the scene."

"Why did you come all the way back here?" Angela asked, with a nervous glance at the kitchen door.

"I can guess Alfred will be the main, perhaps the only, suspect. Since he is Eric's grandfather, like it or not, I thought Marge and Eric should both know right away."

"Thank you," Marge said. Carl spun around and headed back out the door.

Marge and Angela were silent for a moment, staring after him.

"So, will the town's people shrug their shoulders and let Alfred Landon off again? Or will they say the devil finally got his due?" Marge asked.

Angela cocked her head to the side. "It's hard to say. Except for drinking a lot, which evidently led to his abusing Jerry, most of what is said about Alfred's past is gossip and supposition. Carl is more involved this time, though. Being Alfred's son has been a trial for him, and he may decide it is time to go after the old man."

"Will Carl be allowed to investigate, since he is a family member?"

Angela shrugged. "The county officers usually include Carl in on anything happening in Dusty. A murder

29

investigation is a little more serious, though; and you're right. His relationship with Alfred could make a difference."

"Is my grandfather a killer?" Eric asked from the doorway, his voice more timid than Marge could remember ever hearing. "Am I related to a killer?"

Marge moved to Eric, aching to put her arms around him but holding back. He hadn't reached the point of allowing close contact yet, not even if his fear was likely to prove true. What could she possibly say or do to help him handle whatever the possibility did to his self-esteem? "We don't know what happened, Eric. But even if he is, it has nothing to do with who you are."

"Yeah. Right." He turned and shuffled to the bedroom, shutting the door behind him.

Marge stared at the door for a long time. She knew how bad this looked for Alfred. She knew the police liked nothing better than to solve a case quickly, probably more so in a rural area where they seemed to find it easy to sweep their problems under the rug. But, if Eric was going to have to deal with the idea of having a murderer for a grandfather, Marge wanted to be sure it was true.

She dug her cell phone out of her pocket and paused, frowning. Shot point blank in the face? Was Alfred capable of doing that?

"Pete, we have a problem," she said as soon as he answered. She outlined what had happened. "I wouldn't be surprised if Alfred did it, but we have to know for sure. I don't want Eric to have to deal with the weight of his grandfather being a murderer if it isn't true."

The line was silent for a moment. "Marge … you know you are even more out of the loop there than you were in

Michigan when you looked into the deaths in the nursing homes."

"I know. And I also want to get home for Benjamin. But I can't leave things the way they are."

The silence stretched for another moment. Marge heard Pete's deep sigh before he said, "You do what you have to do. Let me know if I can help."

Marge had disconnected before she realized she hadn't asked about Benjamin. She had a feeling Pete had been evasive during their conversation last night, and she wanted to know what was going on. She couldn't let Eric overhear the conversation, though, in case her instinct was right. The boy had enough on his mind without adding worry about Benjamin.

Since Angela was busy with her kids, Marge poured herself a cup of coffee and wandered to the deck at the back of the house. The manicured perfection of the front lawn was not in evidence here. The backyard was trampled, grass nonexistent under the swing set and slide, and children's toys were scattered around. She sat on a lawn chair and leaned her head back, enjoying the comfort of the family disarray and the warmth of the mid-morning sun for a moment. Once she was sure Eric and the other children were playing in Joey's room, she called Pete again.

"I didn't want to worry you," Pete responded to her questions about Benjamin. "No one has seen Ben's mother since she ran away from the rehab facility. Ben wasn't too late last night. I tried to talk to him. He wouldn't say much, but he did tell me he knew she was out, and he intended to look for her. He's afraid if the police find her first they'll lock her up. Of course, he's right. I can't convince him rehab is the best thing for her, and I don't know what he will do if he finds her before we do."

"Can you make him stay home?" Marge asked, but she already knew the answer.

"I could try, and possibly I could even enforce it, although he's a pretty experienced escape artist himself. But I think it would create a huge rift in my relationship with Ben."

"Is he there now?"

Pete called Benjamin to the phone.

"Benjamin, I know this is hard for you," Marge said, "but your mother made her own choices, and she's stuck with them for now. I don't think she would want her choices to ruin your life, too."

Benjamin answered after a moment, his voice strong with conviction, even though it was trembling. "If I don't take care of her, who will?"

"There are professionals who can care for your mom, Benjamin. Even if it doesn't seem like it to you, she is safest when she's in rehab. I hope you can trust me on that. ... Can I talk with Pete again, please? Know I love you."

Pete came back on the line. Marge's voice was too choked up to talk much. She told Pete she would update him regularly about what was happening here and asked him to do the same.

After she disconnected, Marge's mind went around in circles trying to figure out what she should do. It was one thing to say she couldn't leave until she was sure of the truth about Eric's grandfather. It was quite another to have any idea how to go about finding it.

Where should she even start? And how could she

concentrate on what was going on here while she was worried about what Benjamin was doing?

Marge knew going home now wouldn't solve Benjamin's problem. She knew she'd have no more luck keeping him at home than Pete. She'd have to handle what she needed to do here as quickly as possible so she could be there for them both when the inevitable crisis came.

She'd start by reviewing what she knew, which wasn't much. She needed to know more about these people if she was going to have any hope of figuring out who, besides Alfred, might want Dan dead.

If she had understood Carl correctly, Alfred's problem with alcohol, leading to his abuse of Jerry, began soon after his wife died in the fire. Did she die before or after Carl's mother committed suicide? How close together did those two things happen?

It appeared the community blamed Alfred for both deaths, even though they didn't have proof he had caused either of them. She sat up, frowning. Had Alfred cheated on his wife, or was Carl conceived after his wife's death? She didn't feel comfortable asking Angela that type of question about her husband. What about the timing of the other suspected infidelities? Why did Dan decide he needed to confront Alfred, and why would Alfred or anyone else care enough to kill Dan for it?

Maybe Alfred's history had nothing to do with Dan's death, but she wouldn't know until she learned more. Besides, this was Eric's family, and it might be good for him to know more about its history.

"I'm going to the library to do some research," she told Eric a few minutes later. "What do you want to do?"

"Go with you," he said.

"You'll probably get bored."

"No. I'll help."

Marge studied him for a moment. She wasn't sure how much help Eric could be, but she had wanted some bonding time, hadn't she? They'd figure it out.

"Okay, sport, let's go," she said. She informed Angela where they were going.

Angela didn't ask any questions about what Marge hoped to accomplish at the library. "You probably won't want to interrupt your work long enough to come back here for lunch, but I expect you for dinner. We eat at six."

"I feel as if we're imposing," Marge said.

"Nonsense. You are family. You only have to take one look at your son and my husband to know we belong together."

*Your son.* Marge felt her heart swell and she glanced at Eric. He ducked his head as if trying to hide an ear-to-ear grin. What a rare sight. How could she possibly say no after that?

~

A helpful librarian at the Pasco Public Library told Marge all microfilmed records for Benton and Franklin Counties were at the Kennewick Library in Benton County. She also said most newspapers had not been microfilmed but copies were kept in the local libraries. Since success in Kennewick sounded iffy at best, Marge decided to head in the other direction and try her luck with the stored newspapers at the small Dusty Township Library.

"What are you looking for?" Eric asked as they were driving out of Pasco.

"Your family history."

"Why?"

"We need to know more about your grandfather and his relationship with Dan if we're going to find out what happened yesterday."

"You really think that old man didn't kill him?" Eric's voice managed to sound doubtful and hopeful at the same time.

"I think we need to make sure he isn't accused of murder if he is innocent," Marge said.

"Sure looks like he did it, though."

"Yes, it does, which is why it would be so easy not to look more closely. Especially since people seem to think he did some bad things in the past, even though they have no proof."

Marge wished she could be more encouraging, but she didn't want to raise false hope.

~

The inside of the Dusty Township Library was warm and inviting. It was also surprisingly modern. Computers occupied one side of the room, another corner was given over to a reading area for children, with books and educational games scattered about on a rug. Computerized index files could be accessed on a monitor at the front desk.

A woman who might have been in her early forties, with long, strawberry-blonde hair and light-blue eyes approached, giving Eric a startled look.

"Hi, my name is Cynthia. Can I help you find anything?"

"Have you lived in this area most of your life?" Marge asked, with a smile.

"Yes, all my life."

"So you probably know why you recognize this young man."

"He has to be related to Alfred Landon and Carl," Cynthia replied, grinning at him.

Eric frowned and squirmed.

"This is Eric, Alfred's grandson. He is Jerry's son," Marge replied.

Understanding dawned on Cynthia's face. Marge went on to explain her interest in finding out more about the Landon family, both because of the murder and because it was Eric's history. She told Cynthia she wanted to go through old newspapers to see if something in his background might have caused Alfred to shoot Dan. She said she'd also like information about Alfred's wife's death, Carl's mother's death, and anything about Alfred's liaisons with teenagers and married women.

Marge looked up in surprise at Cynthia's derisive snort. "I can help you with those teenagers, but you won't find anything in the newspapers about them," she said.

"Why not?"

"The editor at the time never publicized the trouble teenagers got themselves into. He said he wouldn't be responsible for making their lives more difficult. I went to high school with those two girls, though, so I can tell you what probably happened. Tina had been getting cozy with the mayor's son, who had a major scholarship to Washington State. All of a sudden, she was prancing around the halls between classes, whispering about being pregnant to anyone who would listen, as if it were a secret. No one was surprised. But, even though she acted as though she thought she had landed the big fish, she seemed afraid to name the father. Everyone expected her to get kicked out of school. Before it could happen, she disappeared. The rumor mill buzzed; most people thought her parents made her have an abortion, after which she was sent to boarding school out east. I don't think anyone knows for sure, even now. Her parents never talked about it and they left town soon after Tina."

"Mayor's son? Does Dusty Township have a mayor?"

"Sort of an honorary one. We called him "the mayor" because he came to play lord of the manor in Dusty after retiring from Microsoft with a few million dollars of Microsoft stock. He has done a lot to rebuild the town— kept the library going and spearheaded fundraising for the fire department."

"So, obviously, his son never admitted paternity to Tina's baby."

"No, and he went on to Washington State, which is known for being a party school. Brent is a party animal, and he promptly lost his scholarship. He didn't need it, anyway, considering his father's fortune, and he did manage to graduate, possibly due to a little financial incentive given to the school."

Marge shook her head. This was getting to be more information than she could absorb all at once. "So, why was Alfred Landon connected to the girl and Brent wasn't?"

"Alfred never was connected to Tina, even though everyone started believing the baby was his. I suppose it was possible, but rather a stretch, for Tina to have considered old Alfred a good catch. The booze hadn't destroyed his looks yet, and that same rumor mill announced he had a good-sized life insurance policy on his wife, which might have tempted her. Still, he would have seemed pretty old to a high-school girl. Again, no one knows for sure about the life insurance and he doesn't live as if he has money. I always suspected the mayor had something to do with suspicion landing on Alfred instead of his son. Who easier to blame it on than the town letch?"

*The town letch?* At what point had the town decided he was a letch? But, first things first. "What about the other girl?" Marge asked.

"I'd be surprised if Bethany could know who the father of her baby was. Her parents were very religious, though. I know they would think abortion was a sin; so they left town and I'm sure she had the baby. I don't know if she kept it or put it up for adoption."

Marge was beginning to get the picture, but had to ask anyway. "So, how was Alfred Landon connected to this one?"

"Her parents apparently decided he seduced Bethany, since he was already suspected of seducing Tina. I'm sure the idea of seduction by an older man was more palatable to upright folks like them than the fact she was sleeping with the entire Pasco football team."

"But they didn't make any charges?"

"No. I always thought they didn't want the shame. Or, maybe Bethany wouldn't agree to testify against him."

"So, the two stories sort of fed off each other. And all of this happened after Alfred's wife died?" Marge said.

"Yes. The two girls got pregnant within a year of each other, five or six years after Mrs. Landon died."

"So, why didn't Carl know Alfred might not have been the father of the babies?"

"Carl was only about three years old; so what he thinks he knows comes from the rumor mill. Since he can't deny he is Alfred's son, and Alfred never had anything to do with him, I suspect he is more inclined to think the worst of the old goat. Plus, his grandparents did everything they could to poison his relations with Alfred."

"Do you have copies of area newspapers from the years all this was happening, or are any of them in the microfilm files at Kennewick?" Marge asked. She needed time to process the information Cynthia had given her.

"We never microfilmed our newspapers. I don't think any of the small towns did."

Marge stared at her. "Dusty has a newspaper?"

"Used to. The old owner kept it going as long as he could, but after he died there was no one to take over. The building was falling apart, so it was torn down and never rebuilt. Mr. Martell was talking about starting another paper, but I guess he got too sick to do it."

"But you still have the newspapers from before it closed down?"

"We do," Cynthia said. "And other area papers we continued to collect after we no longer had our own. Tell me the dates you're interested in and I can bring you a storage box or two of all the local newspapers from that time."

"Thank God you have them organized. I'll have to do some figuring to narrow down the date ranges I need."

She looked around to see Eric sitting at a computer not far from her. "Eric, do you know how old your father is?"

Eric looked up, surprise on his face followed by a frown.

"No. We never did birthdays." He turned back to the computer screen, his frown deepening. "I thought public records meant the public could look at them," he said.

"What public records?"

"All these places say free birth and marriage records, and as soon as I get close to finding out anything they say I have to sign up for a free week before I can go further. What happens after the free week?"

"I think you already figured it out. If you don't cancel, they start charging you," Marge said. "Thank you for not signing up, because if you did you'd have to remember to cancel. Why do you want birth and marriage records?"

Eric pulled his head down between his shoulders. "My mom and dad both came from this town. I think they got married here. I never knew her."

Eric seemed more interested in learning about his mother than about Alfred. "We'll make it a point to find out everything we can about her, even if we have to work on it after we get back to Bellevue," Marge promised. It might require a return trip to get enough information to satisfy Eric, but given the family Eric had discovered here, more trips were probably going to happen anyway. She was fairly certain Eric's parents had eloped and married, if they did make it official, after arriving in Seattle.

Picking up a pencil and paper, Marge began making notes. Alfred gets married—when? They have a son, Jerry—how long after marriage? Alfred's wife dies in a suspicious fire—how much later, and how old was Jerry? Five or so years later two teenage girls get pregnant. Carl was about three at the time. So Carl was born about two years after the fire, meaning Alfred's relationship with Carl's mother, whatever it was, could have started a year or two after his wife died. Carl's grandparents said it was a one-sided thing. They claimed Alfred raped and stalked her. Could it have been a consensual affair, instead? At any rate, it somehow made Marge feel better to realize Alfred had probably not cheated on his wife. She wondered when (or if, knowing how the rumors about the teenagers started) the married women had connected with Alfred.

She needed a date to start with. Pulling out her cell phone, she dialed the number Angela had given her.

"How old is Carl?" she asked as soon as she heard Angela's voice.

"What?"

"I'm sorry, that was pretty abrupt. This is Marge. I'm trying to figure out a timeline so I can look up some information. The only firm figure I can get my hands on right now is Carl's age."

Angela laughed. "Carl turned thirty-two last month," she said.

"Thank you," Marge said and hung up. She stared at the phone a moment, realizing she hadn't even said good-bye. Shaking her head, she glanced over to see Eric still busy doing something on the computer before returning to her own calculations.

If Carl was thirty-two, he was born in 1973. Cynthia thought he was about three when the teenagers got pregnant, which was about five years after the fire. So, the fire was probably in 1971. Not knowing how long Alfred had been married, Marge decided to start her search in 1965. If she didn't find what she needed going forward, she'd have to go back a couple of years.

While Cynthia went to retrieve the newspapers from 1965 onward, Marge considered what she had learned from the librarian. Cynthia's revelations made her question everything she had thought about Alfred. Would she never learn not to jump to conclusions or make judgments about people, especially if she didn't have all the facts? For Eric's sake, she needed to have all the facts. She still wasn't convinced they would prove Alfred innocent, but Eric deserved to know the truth.

Cynthia set Marge up at a table in the back of the library.

She had been looking through the newspapers a few minutes before Eric peered over her shoulder. "What are you looking for?" he asked.

"First, your grandparents' wedding announcement."

She had discovered what section of the paper contained the wedding announcements, which made the search a little faster, but she still felt as if it would take her forever to find the information she was looking for.

"Can I help?"

"Well, sure," she said, wondering why she hadn't thought to ask him. She had been a parent of a twelve-year-old boy once before. She should know not to underestimate their intelligence. "You start with 1967. The wedding announcements are usually in this second section of the paper. You don't have to look at other sections unless you don't find announcements there."

Marge found what she was looking for in June of 1966. The picture accompanying the announcement took her breath away. Alfred had, indeed, been a handsome young man. While Carl and Eric both looked remarkably like him, there was something more compelling about his direct gaze. He looked strong, confident, nothing like the broken down old man she had encountered at the farm. His wife, Marilyn, had been equally attractive, but willowy and ethereal. The way he held her in the photo looked protective. They made a stunning couple. Marge printed a copy of the page and handed it to Eric, who studied it with a frown.

"All right, now we're looking for your father's birth announcement. Finding it will be harder because birth announcements don't come with captions and pictures. But they also have the same location in most newspapers; so once we discover where they are posted, it won't be too hard."

She handed Eric a stack of papers from 1969, but before long she found the announcement in August of 1968. She printed it, too. Eric might not be interested now, but this was his history and she would compile it for him.

"Now, it gets harder," Marge told Eric, putting the five years they had searched back in the box and taking out the next three. "We're looking for news articles about your grandmother's death in a fire at the farm."

Marge gave Eric 1970 and she took 1971. She figured a boy with his curiosity would find many things to interest him as he went through the paper, and according to her figuring the fire had happened in 1971.

After only a few minutes, Eric let out a little yclp. "Sweet truck," he said. "Wonder if he still has it around."

Marge looked over to see a photo of a smiling Alfred Landon leaning back against the hood of a Chevrolet pickup, legs crossed at the ankle. He was holding up an impressive string of fish, which the caption identified as trout. She tousled Eric's hair, laughing. "Probably not, but maybe we can peek into his barn and find out," she said.

Still smiling, she went back to her papers and soon found what she was looking for. As Carl had said, Marilyn died in a fire in an outbuilding on the farm. Alfred had told the reporter Marilyn was in the habit of spending time in the building to get away from the demands of life and find some inner peace, and that she often burned candles and incense for their calming effect. Alfred appeared distraught in the photo. The article said the fire was still under investigation.

Marge printed the article and trolled slowly through the next few months, but she found no more mention of the incident. Maybe Carl could check the police files and discover why the investigation had been dropped, or at least not reported on again.

Eric had lost interest and was again engrossed in something on the computer.

Marge wasn't sure what had been written about the rest of the incidents on her timeline, so she had to move slowly as she continued leafing through the papers. She was grateful this was a small town. Even with events relegated to their own section of the paper, she couldn't imagine searching through a large daily like the *Seattle Post Intelligencer* for this kind of information.

An article about a Courtney Whiting's suicide jumped out at her. It showed a picture of a middle-aged couple holding an infant, which proved to be one-year-old Carl Whiting. It also said Alfred Landon had admitted to being the child's father. The photo of Alfred in this article showed a man haggard and worn by life. Was he already drinking? Had he already started taking his anger out on Jerry?

And if he had fathered other children, why did he admit paternity to Carl but not to the others? Was it because Carl looked too much like him to deny?

# SEVEN

~~~~~~~

Not sure what she would find for Eric at the Dusty Café across the street from the library, Marge drove back to Pasco for a late lunch at Wendy's. Taking a bite of her chili, Marge grinned at Eric's choice of a loaded baked potato. She remembered how worried he had looked the first time he tried one, determined to eat whatever Pete ate. Evidently he had discovered it was pretty good. Maybe she should have tried the café after all.

"So, what else did you learn on the computer today?" she asked.

"I was looking up stuff about DNA."

Marge shot him a startled look. She thought he had been playing computer games. How had a twelve-year-old so quickly picked up on Carl's suggestion about DNA having a possible bearing on this case? She'd have to remind herself again not to underestimate his intelligence and intuition.

"And what did you learn?" she asked.

He shrugged. "This one place says it takes three to five days to get the results. I don't know if cops can get it faster. All you need is some spit. I wonder why the old man didn't do it."

Marge wondered whether Eric would ever soften

enough toward Landon to call him grandfather. Did she care? "I don't think the kind of DNA testing we need could be done that fast. We'll have to find out. But, even if they had DNA testing back then, Alfred probably couldn't force the mothers to have the boys tested, and he might not have wanted to attract more attention to himself."

Eric shrugged. "Well, somebody's gotta do it now. How else will they know if the guy who was killed was his son?"

Marge stared at him. Surely Eric was right and the police would do a DNA test on both Dan and Alfred. If it wasn't already in the works, she would mention the possibility of doing it the next time she saw Carl.

As they were walking out of the restaurant, Marge's cell phone rang. "Marge, this is Carl. You don't have to do this, since Alfred won't be any threat to Eric's custody once he's in prison, but he is asking if you still want to talk with him."

"At the Dusty police station?" Marge asked.

"Yes, the county guys parked him here until they're ready to head back to Pasco. He is not exactly sober, and he's a bit shaky, but he is more coherent now and says he'll talk with you. He'll be going to the county jail sometime today. You will have a harder time getting in to see him after he is locked up there."

"Well, we came up here to talk with him. Eric and I are in Pasco right now, but we'll be there as soon as we can."

~

Eric stared out the window during the drive back to Dusty, his fists balled in his lap. "You can leave the room anytime you want," Marge promised, as they walked toward the police station. "But I think you at least ought to see him while he isn't drunk." She could only hope seeing his grandfather in jail wouldn't disturb Eric even more.

Marge also hoped her own jitters wouldn't affect Eric. She kept her hand on his shoulder, guiding him as they followed Carl into the small room where Alfred sat at a scratched-and-weathered table. Two folding chairs had been placed on the opposite side of the table.

"I'll be right outside," Carl said, giving Alfred a warning look before he left the room and closed the door.

Marge gazed at the stoop-shouldered old man. What a difference from the handsome, young groom in his wedding photo. Alfred squinted at them with bleary eyes.

"I'm told I need to apologize to you, even though you almost ran me down," he said in a raspy voice. He looked at Eric and shook his head. "You look so much like your father, habit sort of took over."

Eric frowned. Marge didn't blame him. That was no kind of an excuse for Alfred's behavior.

Looking at Marge, Alfred said, "I promised myself I'd be sober when you came, but I got nervous and decided one drink wouldn't hurt. Of course, I didn't stop at one drink. It won't happen again. I learned my lesson with Jerry and I know I can do better."

He turned his attention to Eric. "You're not exactly like your dad, you know. He had more of his mother in him."

Marge was surprised to see a wistful look pass over the haggard face.

"You're stronger, more like me."

Was he trying to say he beat Jerry because he was too

much like his mother? Did he somehow blame Jerry for his wife's death? Or perhaps Jerry reminded him too much of the woman he had loved. Whatever the reason, and even though Marge knew Eric was a tough kid, she doubted he was tough enough to keep Alfred from lashing out in a drunken rage.

She glanced at Eric to see that his scowl had deepened and his hands were once again balled into fists.

"I'm going to AA as soon as I get out of here. I'll show you I can take care of my grandson," he added, turning back to Marge.

Marge's stomach clenched. How many times had Eric's father made the same promise before CPS terminated his parental rights? She reached out to draw Eric closer to her. It took her a moment to realize he didn't pull away.

It would be useless to argue with Alfred. Anyway, he was delusional if he thought he was going to be released anytime soon, if at all. If he did get out, she could only hope he wouldn't be able to convince the authorities he could stay sober. Since Carl seemed to think it was a foregone conclusion that Alfred was going to prison for murder, why didn't she leave well enough alone?

Instead, she heard herself ask, "Was Dan your son, too?"

Alfred shook his head. "No, he couldn't be. I suppose it was easy enough for his mother to protect his real father by blaming me—but I never touched her. I have no idea why Dan came to the farm." He shook his head. "I wish I had some idea what I was doing when he did."

Marge couldn't think of anything they could accomplish by staying in the room. She began to wonder what had made her think coming was a good idea. Now, though, she didn't think they could leave Dusty until they found out if Alfred had indeed killed Dan.

"Is there anything you want to say?" she asked Eric, before standing up to leave.

At first she thought Eric wouldn't reply. After a moment, he scrunched up his face and blurted, "I'll never live with you, old man; so you can just forget it."

He charged out of the room. Marge almost apologized to Alfred for the outburst before shrugging and following Eric into the hallway. She grasped his shoulders and turned him to face her. "He can just forget it, because it will never happen," she said, hoping she was speaking the truth.

Carl seemed to sense what she was talking about. He took Eric's shoulders from Marge and turned the boy to look at him. "Remember my promise," he said. "You have nothing to worry about."

That made Marge worry a little. If things went wrong, if worse came to worse, to what lengths would Carl go to protect Eric?

As they walked toward the outer office, Carl said, "You had something to tell me?"

Marge looked at Eric, who hung back. "It's your idea," she said. "Ask what you wanted to know."

"Did you do a DNA test on Mr. Landon?"

Well, *Mr. Landon* was better than *that old man*, Marge thought.

"Why would we do a DNA test?"

Marge had the distinct impression Carl was testing Eric's logic, not questioning it.

"Well, I guess you better do one on that man who was

49

killed. And if you do, you need Mr. Landon's, too, so you can find out if they match."

Carl grinned. "Well thought out, young man. You might make a good detective one day. Yes, we have sent in DNA samples from both of them. I'm afraid it will be weeks before we get the results. I don't know why Alfred would have any reason now to lie about being his father, though."

"Did Dan give you any reason why he wanted to see Alfred?" Marge asked.

Carl shook his head. "I made the mistake of assuming I knew, so I didn't question him. But, I can't think of any other reason why he wanted to meet Alfred except that he thought Alfred was his biological father."

"At the time all these women were getting pregnant, did Alfred deny he was the father of their babies?"

"Not to my knowledge," Carl said. "My grandparents might know more, since it all happened when I was a small child."

"I'd like to talk with your grandparents," Marge said.

Carl stood back, narrowing his eyes. "They don't have anything to do with this," he said, his voice suddenly cold.

"You must realize they could have information no one else does. Their information could help us put all the pieces of the puzzle together."

Carl was shaking his head. "My mother's suicide put my grandparents through enough grief. I don't want to dredge it all up again."

Which is why Carl shouldn't be involved in this investigation, Marge thought. Hadn't the county taken over the case?

As soon as these thoughts crossed her mind, she tried to

shove them back. Carl had been more than kind. He had been open and accepting to Eric and her. She couldn't start questioning his right to be involved in this investigation and continue accepting his hospitality.

Once out of the box, however, the thought wouldn't go away. Carl was far too entwined in the threads of the investigation to be able to proceed with an open mind. And since he had accepted Eric and her as family, how was she going to do something she knew he didn't want her to do?

# EIGHT

Carl arrived home in time for dinner. He cocked his head when he saw Marge, a look of surprise on his face. "Since Alfred cannot possibly get custody of Eric now, I thought you'd be heading back to Bellevue," he said.

Marge shook her head. "No, not yet."

"Why do you want to stay around here?"

"Before I let Eric believe he has the blood of a killer in his veins, I want to make sure it is true."

"You have any doubt? Dan was killed a short while after you stopped in to see Alfred. Alfred was already drunk and belligerent to you. He most likely continued drinking; so, of course, he has no memory of where he was or what he was doing. Alfred's shotgun was the murder weapon, we now know for sure. It happened on Alfred's property. After the way Alfred threatened you, how can you think he didn't do it?"

"I didn't say I don't think he could have done it. The problem is, I don't know for sure he did."

"It solves your problem if we leave it as it is," Carl reminded her.

"It also leaves a killer out there if it isn't true," countered Marge.

Carl narrowed his eyes. "You did say you are married to a policeman, didn't you?"

"A homicide detective, yes."

"And he allows you to get involved in his cases?"

Marge squirmed. "I wouldn't say *allows*, exactly."

"Uh-huh. Which means I have a slight chance of telling you to go home and expecting it to happen?"

"That's about it."

"All right, then. You don't need to pay for a motel room for however long it takes you to be satisfied. Eric and Joey can camp out with sleeping bags in Carla's room and you can sleep in Joey's."

"Don't you think you should check with Angela before making such an offer?"

"Huh," Carl grunted. "I thought you'd already be on your way home, so whose idea do you think it was?"

Marge laughed. "In that case, I accept with gratitude. Thank you."

~

There was only one problem with staying at Carl and Angela's home. After the long and stressful day, Marge would have liked to put her feet up and relax with a glass of wine. However, there was no alcohol evident in the house. Even though it appeared Carl didn't drink, given the family's tendency to alcoholism, she thought it was better if she didn't bring any in. Was the alcoholism genetic or had Jerry learned it from his father? Was it one more thing to worry about with Eric?

Once everyone was settled in for the night and Marge assured herself Eric was asleep, she called Pete.

"What is happening with Benjamin?" she asked as soon as she had greeted Pete.

"He's out later tonight. I don't know if he's located his mother. The police haven't. I'm afraid if he finds her before they do, he'll try to take her out of harm's way."

"Like, how?" Marge asked.

"Find some kind of transportation and leave the area."

"But neither of them has any money."

The line was silent.

"You don't think," Marge whispered, "you don't think Benjamin would steal the money to pay for transportation?"

"I think Ben would do anything he thought was best for his mother. The problem is, he doesn't know what is best. Oh, before I forget to tell you, I've been keeping an eye on Jerry Landon, and he has disappeared."

"What? When?"

"No one has seen him since the night before last. If he left during the night or early yesterday morning, he could have been out there in Dusty by the time your murder happened."

"Oh, no," Marge said. "Eric is already feeling tainted by bad blood. How much harder would it be for him if it turns out his father is the killer? But—what possible reason would Jerry have to kill Dan?" Not having an answer, they said good night and ended the call. Marge frowned at the phone in her hand. Why had Pete changed the subject so quickly?

# NINE

After disconnecting, Pete turned back to Olivia. He hated keeping things from Marge, but there wasn't anything she could do to help him, plus she had a lot to handle where she was.

"So, you think Ben found out where his mother is?" Olivia asked, her deep-blue eyes worried.

Pete nodded. "Food is missing. I'm sure he took it to her."

"We need to talk to him about stealing." She appeared agitated, twisting strands of her long, black hair.

"No. If he comes back, I'll talk to him about asking permission, but I'm not going to accuse him of stealing food from his own home. The problem is, he doesn't know how I feel about it. It's possible he is afraid to come home now."

Olivia smiled. "I'm so glad you and Marge have taken the boys into your home and hearts, Pete. I sometimes forget you have become their parents, not just their caretakers." She sobered. "We'll have to hope he does come home so you can make sure he knows how much you care."

Pete had warned Ben he would put his foster care situation in jeopardy if CPS didn't think he would follow the rules. Pete hoped his warning was enough to convince Ben to return at night, but Pete also knew protecting his mother took precedence over anything else in the boy's life.

"Do you have any idea where his mother might be?" Olivia asked.

Pete shook his head. "Everyone is on the lookout for her, but she has evidently gone somewhere she has never used before. I'm hoping Ben will come home for more food and we can either get the information from him or follow him back to her."

Pete heard the back door open. He unclenched fists he hadn't realized were clenched, relief flooding him as he turned to face Ben. The boy didn't look as dejected tonight, but he glanced back and forth from Pete to Olivia as if they were the enemy and he needed to escape.

"Why are you here?" he asked Olivia.

"Because we are worried about you and your mother," Olivia said. "If you can take us to her, we can get her back into a safe situation."

Ben was shaking his head. "If you find her, she'll go to jail," he said. "That will kill her."

"I think her life out there will kill her," Olivia said. "Especially if she has started using again."

Ben shook his head harder. "She ain't using. She told me she's done with that stuff. But if she gives herself up, she'll go to jail." He shot a look of accusation at Pete.

Now it was Pete who shook his head. Marge had always thought Eric was the tough one and Ben easily hurt. In the few months Ben had been a part of their life, Pete had learned Ben could be as tough as Eric if he thought his mother needed protecting. They would accomplish nothing more tonight.

"You know you need to stay home now," Pete said.

"You gonna ground me because I took some food?" Ben asked, his voice as belligerent as Pete had ever heard it.

"No, I'm not grounding you. It's late and well past time for boys your age to be safe, at home." Pete wondered what kind of impact that comment would have on a boy who had spent as many nights on the street as Ben had. "This is your home, and you are always welcome to any food in it."

"Yeah, sure. Can I go to bed now?"

Pete stifled a sigh. "I want to see you here in the morning," he said.

Ben shrugged, his eyes shrouded. He shuffled to his room and closed the door firmly behind him.

When Ben was out of earshot, Pete looked at Olivia as if she could impart some wisdom to help him know how to deal with the boy. This whole thing was new to him, and right now he felt completely over his head.

Olivia gave Pete a quick hug before leaving. "We can only hope that if she isn't using and Ben is feeding her, she discovers she doesn't need gentlemen friends to provide money or drugs," she said. "Otherwise, we definitely can't allow Benjamin to be involved in her life. So, will you have him followed tomorrow, to make sure it doesn't happen?"

Pete nodded. Their first priority was to protect Ben. Pete could only hope Ben would still have trust in their relationship after Pete did whatever he had to do.

# TEN

The doorbell rang at seven o'clock Wednesday morning, followed by a pounding on the door. By the time Marge pulled on jeans and a sweater and went out to see what the commotion was, Angela had already opened the door and the intruder had pushed his way into the house.

"Where is Carl?" he demanded.

"Carl has already gone to work," Angela said.

Marge cringed. Did Angela realize she had told a strange man they were alone with the children? She looked again at the intruder and gasped, realizing why Angela had let him in.

"Jerry!" she looked around for some kind of protection in case she needed it. "What are you doing here?"

Before he could answer, Eric charged out of the children's bedroom. "Dad? Get out of this house! Get out now!" he shouted.

Jerry raised both his hands and backed toward the door, but didn't leave. "Watch your temper, boy, or you'll turn out like your grandpa and me. I'm not here to cause trouble," he added, with a quieter voice. "I saw the murder on the news, and how they arrested my father. I wanted to find out what was going on."

Marge narrowed her eyes, studying him for a moment.

He appeared worn and rumpled, but not drunk. "You left Bellevue before the murder happened," she said.

The look he shot at Marge chilled her.

"Did you kill that man?" Eric demanded before Jerry could say anything.

Marge pulled Eric to her to calm him and waited for further explanation. Instead, she got a question.

"Do you believe the man who was murdered was my brother?" Jerry asked, his voice cold.

Apparently he had been in town long enough to hear all the gossip. "It appears he might be," Marge said.

Jerry snorted. "My father didn't cat around the way they claimed," he said. "Women were all over him, but he only loved my mother. Carl's mother was crazy about my father, and he took to her, but he wouldn't marry her. She killed herself because he rejected her. He probably blamed himself for her death, because after she killed herself his drinking really got out of hand."

"None of which explains why you are here," Marge said.

"I don't have to explain anything to you," he barked.

"So, why *are* you here?" Angela pressed.

Jerry looked from one woman to the other. He grinned a crooked smile that contained no mirth. "So, where was my father's bastard son yesterday morning?"

"Get out of my house," Angela said, her voice tense with repressed anger.

With another grin at the women and a sharp look at Eric, Jerry left.

Marge frowned. The way he asked about Carl indicated he knew exactly where Carl was yesterday. How could Jerry know for certain, unless he was there, too?

Eric turned to Marge. There was no tough guy in his face now. His eyes were wide with fear. "Do you think he came here for me?"

Marge felt herself turn cold. Maybe Eric had a point. The reason Jerry came to the house could have been to verify Eric's presence. If he wanted Eric back, he'd have to kidnap him. Would it be easier to do it in this small town than in Bellevue?

"I hope not, Eric, because he would go to jail for a very long time if he tried to take you," she said, hoping to calm his fears.

He didn't look any more convinced than Marge felt. "And he'd have to deal with me," she added. She was gratified to see an easing of tension in Eric's face.

# ELEVEN

M arge grabbed her cell phone to call Pete while Angela went into the kitchen to call Carl on the house phone.

"If Jerry doesn't think Dan is Alfred's son, he would have no reason to kill him," Pete said. "Assuming inheriting a rundown farm is enough reason for murder in the first place. Are the police doing a DNA test on the murder victim?"

"Yes, and on Alfred, too. I'd also like to see the other presumed son who still lives in Pasco tested, but I can't think of any good reason to ask for it. And, except for the farmhouse itself, the homestead might be worth a lot more than we've considered."

"If I were Alfred, I'd like to have all doubts cleared up as to who might inherit from me," Pete said. "I wouldn't be surprised if he's already done the DNA test."

"I'll ask Carl if we can check. By the way, there is also a rumor Alfred had a life insurance policy on his wife. I wonder if it was large enough for Dan to decide he wanted to inherit some of it—or for someone to murder Dan to prevent him from getting any of the money."

"Marge, tread carefully. I can see you trust Carl, and I trust your instincts, but if Jerry has a reason to murder an interloper, perhaps Carl does, too. It appears neither has an alibi for the time of the murder. Now, before you hang up, let me talk to Eric, please."

"First, any new developments with Benjamin?"

"No. We haven't found his mother yet—but he has. And he won't say anything about her except 'she ain't using.' I'm afraid we're going to have to tail him and hope he leads us to her."

Marge gave the phone to Eric and went into the kitchen to give him some privacy.

"Carl's coming home to talk with both of us and Eric," Angela said, finishing her call as Marge entered the room. She peered at Marge. "I hope you don't make anything out of what Jerry said about Carl. You know Carl couldn't be the killer."

Marge nodded, unable to be more reassuring. Carl, more than Jerry, thought he might be related to the murder victim. Alfred either knew he was or knew he wasn't. So far, no convincing reason for any of them to kill Dan had surfaced. All of them, however, might have had the opportunity.

By the time Carl arrived they had showered, dressed, and eaten breakfast. Eric was much calmer after talking with Pete, and Marge hoped talking with Carl wouldn't spoil it.

"Dan's mother is here now, but she seems indifferent to what the results of the DNA test will show. Since all this seems to be related to the rumors about Alfred, we asked Leroy, the other possible son, to take a DNA test. He informed us he had one done as soon as he came of legal age. He talked his father into doing one, too, even though they both knew their DNA wouldn't match. Leroy couldn't figure out why his mother insisted they keep the truth a secret since the whole town already believed Alfred was his biological father. Leroy confronted her with what he had discovered and she finally admitted her husband was not his biological father, but, even after all these years, she refused to admit or deny if Alfred was."

"Well, if Cynthia's suspicions are right, the two teen-age girls are out of the picture. Jerry seems to think you and he are Alfred's only children. I wonder why, and if it matters."

Carl shook his head. "Whatever the reason Dan went out to the farm, it seems likely Alfred shot him. His are the only prints on his shotgun, which was the murder weapon, and he was so drunk he can't account for his time. Alfred appears ready to take the blame but claims he had every right to protect his property from an intruder." Carl stopped and thought a moment. "How he thinks he can make that fly, I don't know. Dan's body was found too far from the house to be considered a threat and he wasn't armed."

Marge remembered how intimidating Alfred had been, and couldn't help thinking he probably did do it in a drunken fit. In fairness to Eric, though, she couldn't let it go until she could be positive one way or the other. "I wonder how Alfred could have hit Dan point blank in the face when he could hardly hold the gun." She thought for a moment. "If Alfred did shoot Dan because he thought Dan was an intruder, what will happen to him?"

"If he's lucky, he'll be convicted of manslaughter."

Marge shook her head. "Why in the world did Dan go out to the farm? Was it only to meet the man everyone said was his father? Why now, after all these years?"

"I guess we'll never know," Carl said.

Too easy an answer, Marge thought. Too easy to, once again, brush it under the rug.

"So, what are you going to do now?" Angela asked.

"I'd like to talk with Dan's mother. She knows the police are doing a DNA test on Dan. I can't see why she would continue to pretend Alfred is the father if he isn't and she knows it."

Carl checked and found out Dan's body was being held at a funeral home in Pasco, nearby, until it was released and his mother could make arrangements to take him back to Walla Walla for burial. Marge decided to take a chance that Dan's mother would be there.

"I don't think you should go with me," Marge told Eric. He didn't need a grieving mother and possibly a dead body added to his emotional baggage. She hated to leave him behind, though. Was it possible Jerry did plan on grabbing him?

Before Carl left he said he would have a patrolman keep an eye on the house in case Jerry came back. Somewhat reassured, Marge left. She wouldn't be gone long.

~

Marge was relieved to discover she had been right. Dan's mother, looking drained and gray, was at the funeral home. "Good morning," Marge said in a quiet voice, approaching the grieving woman. "My name is Marge Peterson. I'm here looking out for Eric Landon's interests."

"Oh, yes." The woman's voice sagged with defeat. "The legitimate one's son."

"Yes. And Alfred's legitimate son insists Carl was his

father's only illegitimate one. Since the police are having a DNA test done, they will soon know if Alfred is Dan's father. If he's not, why hide the truth any longer?"

The woman looked at Marge for a long moment before sighing and slumping into a chair. "No, Alfred is not Dan's father, and I never claimed he was. That was all town gossip. I let it go on in order to stop any other speculation. I don't understand why Dan went to see Alfred after I told him the truth. He seemed to think he should apologize to Alfred, as if it would make any difference. And I'll never understand," her voice choked. "I'll never understand why Alfred murdered him. None of it was Dan's fault. It's me he should have murdered, for keeping quiet and allowing his name to be slandered all these years."

"You and who else would Alfred blame?" Marge asked in a gentle voice. "Does Dan's real father know about him?"

The woman's face hardened. "That is a locked door. With Dan gone, no one else needs to be hurt."

"Alfred is being hurt," Marge said.

Dan's mother jumped up from the chair and stood in front of Marge, her eyes sparking with anger. "Alfred murdered my son. I don't care why he did it. I don't care if he blames me for ruining his reputation, or if the devil in the drink made him do it. Don't expect me to do anything to help him."

Marge was chilled by the depth of the woman's hurt and hate. "Please accept my condolences for your loss," she managed before leaving the funeral home.

Had she accomplished anything besides angering the distraught woman? Or had she only verified what they would soon know anyway? Once they received the lab results showing Dan's DNA didn't match Alfred's, was there any way to find out whose DNA it did match? They couldn't very well test every male in town. And did it even matter?

Of course, it mattered. Unless they managed to determine Alfred's guilt without a doubt, anyone connected with Dan in any way mattered. And Marge would not be satisfied to blame Alfred for the murder unless they could prove it without any doubt.

Marge decided it might help to look into one other loose end. Leroy had taken the initiative and discovered his legal father, his mother's husband, was not his biological father. Had he decided to take it a step further and find out who his biological father was? If he had, what were the chances it was the same man who was Dan's biological father?

Before trying to figure out how to follow up with Leroy, Marge pulled out her cell phone and called Angela to make sure Eric was still safe.

"Hi, Angela. How's Eric doing?"

"Oh, I was about to call you," Angela said, her voice high. "The kids were playing in the backyard. When I went to get them for lunch, Joey told me Eric took off about half an hour ago and made him promise not to tell me he was gone."

Marge's heart lurched. Words came babbling out of her mouth as soon as they entered her head. "Took off? You mean ran away? Why would he run away? Where would he go?"

"Joey said Eric was talking about keeping us safe. Do you suppose he thinks Jerry will be a danger to us if he stays here?"

The idea of Eric running away in order to protect his new family was so like him it somehow settled Marge's thinking. "My guess is that is exactly what he is worried about." In fact, it was so like him, Marge felt a twist of guilt. Why hadn't she considered the possibility and brought Eric with her?

"But where would he go in a town he doesn't know?" Angela asked. "He didn't tell Joey anything. Joey said they were having fun tossing the football around. All of a sudden, Eric dropped it, said he had to leave, swore Joey to secrecy, and took off."

"Eric has spent a good amount of time on the streets. He knows how to take care of himself. Pasco is pretty small for hiding in, though, and I don't know how well he could adapt to living out in the country." At least it is summer, she thought. They didn't have to worry about him being cold.

"Well, I'm going to hang up now and call the county police department to try and get them to start a search for him," Angela said. "Most of the officers grew up around here, so they should have some ideas about where he might try to hide."

Even knowing it was probably useless, Marge couldn't help getting into her Honda and driving up one street and down the other, peering into store fronts and down alleyways, hoping if Eric saw her he would come to her.

He wouldn't, though. If he thought it was a danger to Carl's family for him to stay there, he'd think it was doubly so for Marge if he was with her. Who would Jerry be more likely to hurt than the person he blamed for taking his son?

After two hours of fruitless driving around, Marge pulled to the side of the road and grabbed her cell phone.

As soon she heard Pete's voice, she lost control and started sobbing. It was a few minutes before she could quiet her sobs enough to tell Pete about Eric.

"Why did I come here? What have I done?" she cried.

"I'm on my way," Pete said.

"But what about Benjamin?"

"Olivia and Robert can handle things at this end for now. I'll be there as soon as I can."

Marge couldn't sit around waiting for Pete to come and rescue her. She dried her eyes, took a deep breath, and started the car.

Pete's voice had steadied her enough to make her realize driving around town aimlessly wasn't getting her anywhere. She pulled into a gas station to refill her tank and paced around the car. Eric could take care of himself. She knew he could. If he stayed out of his father's reach, he would be all right.

But what if Jerry had been watching the house and picked Eric up? Was Jerry taking him as far out of town as he could, as fast as he could? They needed to keep tabs on Jerry. If Jerry didn't have Eric it meant Eric was still hiding out somewhere and she could believe he would be all right until they got things sorted out. When she found Eric, she was taking him home immediately. She could not put him in jeopardy to satisfy her own compulsion to find the truth.

~

"Carl, do you have a BOLO out on Jerry?" Marge asked as soon as she had him on the phone.

"No. The Pasco police are looking for Eric. They have one out on him."

"Eric can take care of himself—as long as Jerry doesn't have him," Marge said. "We need to find Jerry."

"Do you think Jerry would take Eric in order to harm him?"

"No, of course not. He'll take Eric because Eric is his son. Jerry thinks he has a right to take him. He won't harm Eric as long as he is sober—but he can't stay sober. Once Jerry is drunk, who knows what he will do? And, sober or drunk, if Jerry found Eric, he is getting as far away from here as he can, as fast as he can. We need to find him."

"Do you know what kind of car he drives?"

"No."

"All right, I'll check out at the Landon house. If his car isn't there, I'll check DMV for the details and put out the word to keep an eye out for it. If we see it, we can stop him and ask if he knows Eric's whereabouts, but we don't have any reason to put a BOLO out on Jerry."

Marge rubbed her forehead. Of course, Carl was right. Eric had run away. As far as they knew, Jerry hadn't found him. Still, she needed to be sure Jerry didn't have Eric now.

"Pete's on his way here," Marge said.

The line was silent for a moment. "If he's coming as a concerned parent, fine. You both need to remember this is not his jurisdiction, though."

After disconnecting, Marge stared at the phone. Of course they knew this was not Pete's jurisdiction. Why would Carl make a point of saying that? Did he have something to hide?

# TWELVE

Even though Eric disappeared in Pasco, Marge felt compelled to head to Dusty. While she was on her way there, Carl phoned to tell her he'd sent his deputy out to the farm and he had not seen Jerry's car. Marge was afraid that might mean Jerry was in Pasco looking for Eric or already had him and was on his way out of the area.

Despite Carl's report, she wanted to check the homestead herself before returning to Pasco. When she drove up to the house, she was stunned to see an ancient, green Chevy Impala sitting in the driveway. Had Jerry been gone when the deputy checked or did the deputy not do what he said he had? Maybe Jerry found Eric and returned with his son after the deputy did his drive-by? It didn't seem like a smart thing to do, but who knew what Jerry was thinking? Marge glanced into the Impala on her way to the front door, but saw nothing out of the ordinary.

"What are you doing here?" Jerry barked, opening the door to her knock.

Marge stepped back to avoid the wave of alcohol emanating from the open doorway. So much for his vow to stay sober. She threw up a quick prayer for forgiveness at the ungenerous thought, but his failure indicated he probably hadn't been in any condition to go to Pasco, find Eric, and bring him back here. It also meant he wouldn't be able to stop Eric's adoption.

"I'm looking for Eric," she said, her voice weak.

Jerry planted his fists on his hips and stared at Marge with narrowed eyes. "You lost my son?" he finally asked in a hoarse whisper. His voice rose. "Are you telling me you lost my son?"

Marge struggled to get the words out. "Is he here?"

Jerry shook his head and stared at his feet. "You lost my son." His voice had become soft again, disbelieving. He raised his head, his face creasing into a wicked grin. "I wonder what those bitches at CPS will think about *that*." He slammed the door in her face.

While he had sounded surprised, Jerry would hardly admit to Marge he had Eric. But, if Eric *was* with Jerry, why were they still here, where people would obviously look?

Was Jerry lying? Did he have Eric hidden somewhere? Marge stepped down off the porch and walked toward her car, looking around the homestead as she did. In addition to the house, there were three weathered outbuildings; they all looked as if they would collapse in a strong wind. One was a garage. One was a barn. The third, closest to the house, seemed to be some kind of tool shed. A shadow moved across a window in the house. Probably Jerry, watching her. She didn't dare look into any of the buildings.

She got in her car, shut the door, and pulled a pen and notepad from her purse. She wrote down the license plate and description of Jerry's car. Feeling safer now that she was back in her blue Honda, Marge pulled out her cell phone. Still no signal. She backed out until she reached the end of the driveway, where two bars jumped into view. She stopped and called Carl.

"You were right. We didn't need a BOLO on Jerry," she said. "Jerry is at Alfred's farm. He must have been gone when your deputy checked because his car is parked right in front of the house. Maybe he was in Pasco looking for Eric.

"He seemed surprised about Eric being missing, but I don't know Jerry well enough to know if he could fake it. Can we get a search warrant?"

"Marge, the judge wouldn't issue a search warrant for the house when Alfred shot Dan because he said everything connected to the crime, including Alfred, were outside the house. I doubt we have enough evidence Eric might be in the house to get one now. Jerry probably didn't even know Eric was missing until you told him. But, to satisfy you, on the off chance Eric is there, we might not need a warrant to get in."

"What do you mean?"

"Jerry doesn't own the farm, Alfred does. I'll call the county jail to see if Alfred will give us permission to search."

As Marge disconnected, she looked up and saw the door to the house open. Jerry emerged and stood on the porch, arms crossed, glaring at Marge. She backed the rest of the way out of the driveway and drove down the road until scrubby bushes and trees prevented Jerry from being able to see her. She stopped the car to wait for Carl to call her back. Of course the trees and bushes also obstructed her view of the house.

Marge put her head down on the steering wheel; a feeling of helplessness engulfed her. How could she have let this happen? She knew Eric would not want to worry her. But, as resourceful as he was, he had no way to contact her, to let her know if he was all right. Once Eric was safely back with her, she would get him a cell phone.

Because she *would* find him.

Her phone rang and she quickly answered it.

"Alfred had no objection to signing an authorization for us to enter his property. The county is faxing it to us right now. As soon as we get it, we'll drive out there."

~

It felt to Marge as if hours had passed before she saw Carl's police vehicle and two county cars turning in at the Landon farm. She made a U-turn and followed them up the driveway. Jerry came to the door, acting belligerent until Carl presented him with the papers. He looked puzzled for a moment before he visibly deflated and moved aside.

Marge stepped out of her car and started walking toward the house. Spotting her from the porch, Carl came back down the steps and put out his hand. "You stay here, Marge," he said. "We have permission from Alfred to search, but this is police business and you can't be part of it."

Marge nodded and stepped back toward her car. As hard as it was, she knew Carl was right. As she watched him go into the house, she realized the police were probably too busy with their search to pay much attention to her—as long as she stayed out of their way. She slowly made her way toward the barn. As she rounded the side of the house, she thought she saw movement near the foundation. She blinked twice and stared at a small head emerging from a basement window. It was Eric! What was he doing in the basement of the house? Before Marge had time to register what she had seen, Eric scooted into the tool shed. He had not seen her.

*The little fox!* Her mouth opened in astonishment. Jerry hadn't kidnapped him. Eric was hiding in his grandfather's house, right under his father's nose. How had he traveled the twenty or more miles from Pasco in such a short time? If Jerry had no reason to go into the basement, it was the safest place Eric could be. And if Eric waited until Jerry drank himself into a deep sleep, it would be easy to get the food and water he needed.

Did she want Eric to be found? If Jerry didn't know where Eric was, Eric was safe, probably safer than if he were at Carl's house. But could she be sure Jerry wouldn't go into the basement? What would happen if he woke from a drunken stupor and found Eric in the kitchen? Would he lash out, as he so often had in Bellevue?

She pulled out her cell phone. "Pete?" she said in a near whisper. "Have you left home yet?"

"No." Pete's voice sounded frustrated. "Olivia can't stay with Ben today, and she says she doesn't think we should risk taking him out of the county. Eric was different because it was to meet his grandfather."

"Don't worry about it," Marge said. "I know where Eric is, and I'm trying to decide what to do about it. He seems to be doing a good job of taking care of himself, but he may be in a dangerous situation."

Marge explained to Pete what Eric was doing. The line

was silent for a moment before he burst into laughter. "I agree, we have one mighty smart boy," he said. "But you can't leave him there."

"What if I can get him away from here without anyone seeing us? No one will think to look for him with me."

"No, it's time for you to bring Eric home. I don't see any way you can keep him safe while you do your investigating. And I also can't condone you wasting the police time and effort to search for Eric when he is no longer missing."

Marge's breath caught in her throat. She hadn't thought about what impact her actions would have on the police. Skirting the edge of the law was okay if she was the only one who might get hurt. "Gotta hang up," she whispered as the officers came out of the house.

Marge hugged herself, trying to release the tension building up in her shoulders. Before the police had cleared the porch, she saw Eric slip out of the tool shed and around to the side. He glanced back. His eyes widened as he caught sight of Marge. He started to straighten up, as if to give up and come to her, but she held up her hand to stop him. With a quick flash of a grin, he scooted to the back of the garage and from there behind a large oak tree. While the police concentrated on the three outbuildings, Eric crawled back to the house and re-entered through the basement window.

Marge closed her eyes and took a deep breath. They wouldn't find him now. All she had to figure out was how to get Eric out of there and how to call off the search.

"No sign of him," Carl said, approaching Marge after the police had completed their search. "Not too surprising, since we knew he ran away and this is quite a distance from Pasco. Jerry didn't abduct Eric from my house and drive him here. It's a good thing we didn't need a search warrant because there were no grounds for believing Jerry was holding Eric against his will." He gave Marge a stern look, as if it were all her fault. Which, truth be told, it was. "It's also a good thing I didn't cancel the BOLO on Eric."

Marge bit her lip. She couldn't ask them to rescind the BOLO without a good reason. However, she didn't need to, since Eric was right here where they wouldn't find him. She hoped she could get him to a safer place before the police wasted too much time searching for him.

Marge dutifully followed the police cars down the road away from the Landon farm and into Dusty. Once they reached town, however, she took a few side streets to turn herself around and head back out to Alfred's farm. A few hundred feet after passing the driveway, she pulled into a two-track. It petered out at the vineyard after going around a small hill, effectively hiding the Honda from the road and the farmhouse.

She wrote a note to Eric, telling him where the Honda was and instructing him to go there if he didn't see her. Stowing her purse in the trunk and leaving the car unlocked, she turned her cell phone to vibrate and put the phone, the note, and the keys in her pocket. Grabbing a flashlight in case this took a while, she hiked through grapevines, arriving hot, scratched, and sticky in back of the barn where she couldn't be seen from the house.

"I should have thought of bug spray," she complained, wiping sweat from her face and slapping at hovering mosquitoes.

Peering around the corner of the barn, Marge could see

the garage between her and the house. She quickly moved up to take a position behind it where she couldn't be seen from the house or the driveway.

*Now what?* she wondered. She couldn't get any closer for fear Jerry would glance out the window on this side. She'd have to hunker down and wait until dark.

Her stomach growled, reminding her she hadn't eaten anything since breakfast. "You're such a great detective," she whispered to herself. "You could have taken the time to pick up a sandwich." She didn't know what made her more miserable, her clammy skin being attacked by insects or her stomach demanding food.

After what seemed like hours, but a quick check of her watch proved to be only thirty minutes, Marge heard the front door slam shut. Peering around the corner of the garage, she saw Jerry lurch to his car. Marge held her breath, watching as he gunned the motor to back out of the driveway, spewing gravel and grinding gears as he turned and sped down the road. While she hoped he would stay away long enough for her to connect with Eric, she didn't want Jerry to end up wrapped around a tree.

No longer needing to conceal her presence, Marge stood and ran to the basement window where she had seen Eric emerge earlier. It was closed, locked from the inside. She rapped on the glass.

"Eric," she called in a loud whisper. Somehow the feeling of stealth made it difficult to shout. "Eric," she called a little louder, rapping on the glass again, with no response. Had he heard Jerry leave? Had he already gone upstairs to get some food? Even though Jerry had left, she couldn't make herself shout any louder.

Marge stood and ran to the front of the house, up the porch steps, and was in the house before she realized Jerry had left the door unlocked. Where would Eric be? Probably in the kitchen. Where was the kitchen? Marge headed down the hallway toward the back of the house and was rewarded by the sight of an open pantry door.

"Eric," she said, still whispering.

He spun around, startled. "What are you doing here?"

"I need to get you out of here," she said.

"No. You don't know what he's like when he's drunk. He don't have no control. If he comes for me, he'll hurt anyone who gets in his way."

"I'm taking you back home," Marge said. At Eric's obstinate look, she added, "Pete says we don't have any choice."

A fleeting look of indecision was followed by the sound of the front door opening. Marge stared at Eric. "Already?" she breathed.

Eric grabbed a jar of peanut butter in one hand and her hand with the other, dragging her to the basement door. He handed the jar to her and opened the door, lifting it slightly as he did. Marge moved down two steps before Eric's hand on her arm stopped her. He closed the door as carefully as he had opened it and motioned her to go on. The next step squeaked under her weight. They froze. A moment later they heard the groan of the dilapidated sofa. They both released their breath at the same time. Marge nearly laughed with relief. Jerry hadn't heard them.

"The booze store ain't far, so he's never gone long," Eric whispered after they reached the bottom of the stairs and he led her to a musty room filled with boxes. Marge had to hold her nose to keep from sneezing. "That door makes a loud noise if you don't hold it up, and that one step always squeaks so you got to close the door before stepping on it."

"You figured out a lot in a short time," Marge said. Eric ducked his head at the praise before noticing Marge look longingly at the jar of peanut butter he held. With a grin, he reached behind her and pulled out the dry remains of a loaf of bread and a dirty table knife. Marge wasn't going to complain. She accepted the sandwich he put together for her with gratitude.

Marge concentrated on chewing and swallowing. The sandwich took the edge off her hunger, but she could have used a bit of water to wash it down. It gave her a new appreciation for what Eric and Benjamin endured when they were out on the streets.

"How do we get out of here?" she asked after she swallowed her last bite.

Eric looked at the window and at Marge. "Not that way," he said.

Marge looked at the window. He was right. She didn't carry any extra weight, but her five-foot-six-inch frame was too much to go through the small opening.

"We'll have to wait until we know he is asleep and go out the front," Marge said.

Eric shook his head. "Not the front. He sleeps right there in the living room. We gotta use the back door, from the kitchen. Once he passes out, we might be safe, but it's still risky."

"We *might* be safe? Is the back door risky, too?" Marge asked.

Eric nodded. "It makes a pretty loud noise when you open it. That's why I used the window."

"Okay," Marge said, amazed at how much she was depending on this twelve-year-old boy to get them out. "So, now we wait until he falls asleep?"

Eric nodded. "A little longer, to be sure he is really under." He walked away and started to search through the clutter in a corner of the small room.

"What are you looking for?" Marge asked. The dust he unsettled was tickling her nose.

"A bag or a box easy to carry," he said. "I found some stuff I want to look at." He looked at her, his expression defensive. "It's not stealing. He's my grandfather, and it's family stuff."

While Marge wasn't good at splitting hairs, it was the first time Eric had referred to Alfred as his grandfather. She thought the idea of Eric having the opportunity to see any of his family history was a good idea. "You can't keep it unless your grandfather agrees," she said. "However, let's go ahead and borrow it for now."

With a relieved grin, Eric dug around until he found a burlap bag. Going to a corner of the room, he proceeded to fill it with what looked like picture albums and old letters. He must have been doing a lot of searching while he was hiding to gather all this "family stuff." Marge hoped he would share it with her later, but it would have to be his decision.

Soon the rumbling of inebriated snoring was loud enough to be heard in the basement. It was time to leave. Leading Marge, Eric tiptoed carefully up the steps, avoiding the one that squeaked. He lifted and opened the stairwell door to the kitchen, but stopped and held up a hand to keep Marge from going through. He waited a full five minutes. Marge was tense from holding her position before she heard the deepening of the rumble from the living room and once again appreciated Eric's wisdom.

Finally Eric motioned for Marge to follow and they slipped through the kitchen to the back door. Eric paused, taking a couple of deep breaths, so Marge did the same. Giving Marge a warning look, he threw open the door and darted out. Marge almost faltered at the loud screeching. She didn't have time to worry about it though. The rumbling stopped abruptly as she followed Eric out and they raced toward the garage.

"Who's there? Who's out there?" Marge heard as she and Eric reached the garage and ran around the corner, panting. When she caught her breath, Marge glanced around the corner. Jerry loomed in the kitchen doorway. She could only hope he would be disoriented in his drunken state and not follow them.

They took a few moments to steady their breathing before Marge stuck her head around the corner again. She blinked. Jerry was holding a shotgun to his shoulder and swinging it back and forth. He must have kept it beside the door. Two loud blasts shook the silence and scattered shot on the other side of the garage. Now was their chance. He would have to reload.

Marge grabbed Eric's hand and, half crouching, scurried toward the barn. Once they were on the other side, she looked back again. Jerry was still struggling to push more shells into the shotgun. She grinned at Eric and they slipped away from the barn and into the vineyard. Every snap of a branch made Marge jump and check to be sure Jerry wasn't following. It seemed to take so long to get to the Honda she was almost convinced they were going in circles.

Once they were in the car and Marge could breathe normally again, she pulled out her cell phone and called Pete. "Okay," she said. "I have Eric and we are out of the house. What now?"

"You head back to Bellevue," Pete said.

"I don't think so," Marge answered. "I haven't finished what I need to do here."

"The most important thing is to get Eric to safety. And Ben needs you, too."

Marge's chest felt tight. Was she being fair to Benjamin? But he had Pete and Olivia to look after him, and Eric only had Marge to sort out his situation. "Can you meet us in Yakima tomorrow?" Marge asked. "Eric and I can get there tonight. After you have Eric, I can return to finish what I need to do."

Silence.

Marge knew Pete was digesting what she had suggested and trying to figure out how much he could sway her position. She heard him speak to someone in the background.

"I'll meet you in Yakima tonight. Olivia just got here and she says she can wait for Ben and stay with him after he gets home." Marge could read the "if" in his pause. She could almost see the shake of his head before he continued, "After I get there, we'll decide what to do next."

Marge found herself nodding even though Pete couldn't see her. She knew he wasn't convinced, but it was the best she could do for now. Before Pete arrived at the motel, she needed to think of some way to persuade him to let her finish what she had started. Marge said good-bye to Pete and ended the call.

"What?" Eric's voice came out in a small explosion.

Marge suspected he had been holding it in ever since he realized he was being sent back to Bellevue.

"There's nothing else to do, Eric. I can't let you hide out on your own. We can't put Carl's family in jeopardy. And we can't afford two motel rooms."

"I was doing okay where I was," he objected.

"Two problems," Marge said as she guided the Honda backward out of the two-track and turned toward the highway to Yakima. "Your father appears to be staying totally smashed. If he found you, who knows what he would do? And, if CPS ever discovered we left you to fend for yourself, especially in the same house as your father, do you think they would trust you to us?"

Eric hunched down in his seat, hugging his bag of treasures between his legs.

What was going on in his busy little head? Marge wondered. If he wasn't convinced to go back home now, she hoped Pete could convince him. Because if this boy decided he needed to be somewhere, he would find a way to be there.

# THIRTEEN

After a silent and tense hour-and-a-half drive to Yakima, Marge found a Wal-Mart where she could buy fresh clothes for both of them, cola for Eric, and a long-overdue bottle of wine and a corkscrew for herself. She reserved a suite in a motel where they took quick showers, changed clothes, and ordered pizza before she called Pete to tell him where they were.

"I'm halfway there," Pete said after Marge gave him the name of the motel. "I'll arrive in an hour or so."

Marge decided she needed to call Angela and tell her what was going on. "I'm not sure there was really any danger, but I wanted to be out of the area before letting anyone know I had Eric," she said. "I hope you can forgive me for making you worry, but I called as soon as I could. Please let Carl know Eric is with me. I don't want the police wasting any more time and effort looking for him."

"I'm relieved to know you both are safe," Angela said, her voice sounding cool. "Does this mean you are going back to Bellevue?"

"I don't think so. Pete is meeting us here in Yakima. He suggested I go home, but there are still too many unanswered questions. I don't want them hanging over Eric's head. Eric is going home, though."

"Let me know what you decide. Your room will be waiting for you, unless you tell me to ship your belongings to Bellevue," Angela said.

Something in Angela's voice made Marge wonder if she was really welcome to return or if Angela was only doing what she felt was her duty. Marge didn't want to insult Angela by questioning her now. She'd have to give it some thought later, when her head was clearer.

After Marge finished her calls, Eric thrust a bundle of envelopes at her. "If you're gonna go back, you can take these," he said, his voice sullen. "They're just a bunch of letters."

Marge took the envelopes and set them aside. She moved behind Eric to look over his shoulder as he thumbed through a photo album.

"That must be your grandmother when she was a teen-ager," Marge said, pointing at a faded photo. Marilyn hadn't changed much as she aged. The picture of the young Marilyn showed the same innocent, slightly shattered look she had as an adult.

"Here's a later picture of her. The baby must be your father." What struck Marge was the disconnect between mother and child. Marilyn's arms looked stiff holding Jerry, and she gazed, unfocused, into the distance. Marilyn appeared to be slightly removed from the scene. How had the lack of warmth affected baby Jerry?

The last photo showed Marilyn and Alfred, slightly older than the wedding picture in the newspaper, but Alfred had the same protective air about him, the same adoration in his gaze.

"I don't know these people," Eric said. He closed the

album and shoved it at Marge, his eyes squinted as if holding back tears. "You can take this back, too. It has nothing to do with me."

The pizza arrived, and the two of them became busy making up for their lack of a proper meal all day. By the time Pete joined them, only a couple globs of cheese stuck to the box.

"I'm sorry," Marge said. "Shall we order another one?"

Pete laughed, wrapping her in a big hug. "Only if you two are still hungry. I brought food to eat on the way." Reaching out a long arm, he pulled Eric close, too. Marge's eyes misted at the easy contact between the two of them.

"You aren't seriously planning on going back there, are you?" Pete asked Marge.

"I think I have to. There is no danger to me, and we need to clear up anything to do with Eric's family."

Eric mumbled into Pete's side.

"What?" Pete asked, holding him away.

"You are my family," he said, looking down as if afraid they would correct him.

Before Marge could worry about how Eric would react, she found herself reaching out and pulling him close. Much to her relief, he didn't pull away.

"We certainly are," she said. "And I'm going to do everything I can to make sure nothing changes that."

"I can help," Eric said. "I want to go with you."

Marge shook her head. "You had to meet your grandfather and we had to determine if he had any claim on you. We now know he doesn't. You're still in foster care, and we have no reason to keep you out of King County any longer."

He turned to Pete, his eyes pleading.

"Sorry, buddy," Pete said. "Marge is right. Besides, Ben needs you."

Eric's face softened into the first hint of a smile Marge had seen since they started for Yakima. "Yeah, Benji can't manage very long without me."

Pete looked hard at Marge. "You didn't tell him anything?"

Marge shook her head.

Eric's eyes swiveled from Pete to Marge and back. The smile was gone, replaced by a stony set to his chin. "Tell me what? Is it about Benji?"

Pete sighed. "Yes. Ben's mother ran away from rehab. Ben has discovered where she is but he won't tell us because he knows if the authorities find her she will be locked up."

"I'm sorry, Eric," said Marge. "You couldn't do anything while we were here, so I didn't want to worry you."

"Can we go home right now?" Eric asked, looking at Pete. "I can help you, and … and …" He looked at Marge. "And Aunt Marge can go back to finish stuff in Dusty."

Marge figured "Mom" would be a longer time coming since she had eroded his trust a little by keeping information about Ben from him.

"No," Pete said. "I need sleep before driving back. We'll go in the morning." He turned to Marge. "The murder has nothing to do with us. Can't you leave it for the local police to handle?'

Marge squirmed. Logically, Pete made sense. Except it appeared everyone had decided Alfred committed a murder she was more and more convinced he hadn't. And, even though she was elated Eric now considered them to be family, Alfred was his biological grandfather. Eric would still feel tainted by bad blood if she couldn't prove Alfred was innocent.

While Marge was certain she had not heard the last about it from Pete, they let it drop for now. They pulled out the sleeper-sofa in the living room for Eric. He was soon fast asleep.

"Have I done anything you think might jeopardize our suitability as parents for Eric?" Marge asked as soon as they were alone in the bedroom.

"Olivia thinks not. Eric running away could have been a problem, but no one in King County actually needs to know about it."

"Unless Jerry decides he wants to make trouble and contacts CPS," Marge said.

"If worse comes to worst, we might have to ask Eric to explain why he ran. Since it was to protect you and the others, I don't think it will reflect badly on our relationship with him."

Reassured, Marge relaxed into the comfort of Pete's arms. The downside to returning to Benton County was the thought of being separated from this man for any longer than absolutely necessary.

"Is there anything new with Benjamin and his mother?" she asked.

"Not so far. We have all kinds of people trying to track Ben, but he's fully aware of it and evidently has more street smarts than we gave him credit for. They can trace his movements to the bus station, where they are sure he takes a bus to Seattle, but he always gives them the slip and they haven't been able to spot him getting on or off a bus. We are now concentrating the search for both Ben and his mother in Seattle."

"Is he spending a lot of time with her?" She tried to brush aside a stab of pain. The woman was Ben's mother, after all. She couldn't blame him for choosing to take care of her.

"Most of the day. He is getting home well past curfew every night, but I haven't wanted to make an issue of it since he does come home." He paused. "He hadn't come home yet tonight when I left. Olivia thinks he is smart enough to know they won't be able to elude capture forever. He might be trying to find a way to get them both out of the county, or even the state."

Marge stifled a sob. Would Eric be any safer at home than he had been in Dusty? She would bet he'd be out on the streets looking for Benjamin as soon as he could get away from Pete. Despite the danger for Eric, she couldn't help thinking he had a better chance than anyone else of finding Benjamin. She knew she had no way to help with that. She could only hope to discover what she needed to as soon as possible so she would be there for Benjamin when he needed her.

~

Pete and Eric left at seven-thirty Thursday morning. Marge decided to have a relaxed breakfast and leave a little later. Over coffee, she flipped through the photo album. It contained no more photos after the one of Marilyn and Alfred. Even though additions to the album appeared to end with Marilyn's death, Marge was sure Marilyn never maintained it. It could only have been Alfred. Studying the photo, Marge wondered what loving so completely a woman who might have been incapable of love had done to a man as strong as Alfred once appeared to be. Had her lack of warmth been the impetus to start him on the road to alcoholism?

Rifling through the envelopes, Marge sorted them by date. The first three were dated a few years after Marilyn's death. They were from Courtney Whiting to Alfred. Carl's mother. Marge read through them twice, frowning. Why had Alfred never produced these letters, in which Courtney begs him to get past his grief and marry her? In the last letter, written the same week she committed suicide, she says she can't go on without him. He let everyone believe he had stalked and abused her, even though his only crime had been rejecting her.

The other letters were written years later, obviously from a young woman in love. Hearts dotted the letter i and x's and o's graced the bottom of the pages. Had Eric looked at these? They were from his mother, Elaine, to his father, and were filled with the kind of romantic nonsense teenage girls were prone to. The last of these letters confirmed plans to run away to Seattle with him and get married. From the date of Eric's birth, Marge suspected Elaine was already pregnant. She died in childbirth, Marge knew, and always suspected Jerry took out his grief on Eric.

Those three letters from Courtney convinced Marge she needed to talk with Courtney's parents.

# FOURTEEN

It was mid-morning by the time Marge neared Dusty. She had spent the entire drive debating with herself about what she was doing. Even if looking for the truth about Alfred's involvement in Dan's death was the right thing to do, how was she going to go about it? She breathed in and out deeply a few times to clear her mind and focus on how to proceed.

Before Eric ran away, she had been planning to locate Leroy and find out what he knew about the identity of his biological father. It still sounded like a good plan. After she talked with Leroy, she'd seek out Carl's grandparents. No matter how unhappy it made Carl, she needed to find out what they knew.

Pulling over to the side of the road, she took another deep breath and called Carl. After apologizing once again for leaving town with Eric before letting Carl and Angela know he was safe, she asked, "Carl, could you put me in touch with Leroy?"

"Why?" Carl asked. "He already told us everything he knows."

"I'm wondering if he would be willing to have his DNA compared with Alfred's, and also with Dan's."

"I'm not sure what Leroy's relationship with Alfred or

Dan has to do with Dan's murder, even if it turns out Alfred isn't Leroy's father. Besides, it probably wouldn't help to compare Leroy's with Dan's. The number of different DNA possibilities increases with brothers, especially when they have different mothers, so the chance of getting a reliable match is slim even if they are related."

"We can try. The question of whether those two are really Alfred's sons may well have a bearing on the case. I'm also pretty sure Leroy would be interested in finding out if Alfred is his biological father."

The line was silent a moment. "All right, I'll ask Leroy if he wants to compare them. But I don't know what interest he would have in talking with you."

"Will you ask?"

"Oh, all right. I'll ask him that, too."

Marge was barely back on the road to Dusty before Carl called back. She pulled over again to answer her cell phone.

"You were right. Leroy is very interested in finding out if Alfred is his biological father. He also wants the brother test done, on the chance Alfred isn't his father and something might indicate whether he and Dan could be related. However, as I said, relationship of brothers with the same father but different mothers is pretty difficult to prove through DNA testing."

"I know. It would be a lot easier if the mothers would open up about what happened. I don't suppose there is any way to force the issue."

"None. Nor would I want to if there were. It's Leroy's business if he wants to find out who his father is, but I see no reason to bring up difficult memories for these women who have had enough pain in their lives."

"Even if it could lead us to why Dan was murdered? And who killed him?"

"We know who killed him and the old goat didn't need a reason, as drunk as he was."

Marge no longer had any reason to get in touch with Leroy, so she would go on to the next step. If Carl was irritated with her now, Marge could imagine how he was going to feel after she did what she planned to do next. If she'd had any doubts about remaining in his home, it was time to forget them.

~

Marge had looked up Carl's grandparents' address the last time she was in the library. As she approached it, she maneuvered her Honda onto gravel and finally dirt roads before she reached the farmhouse, which was as far out in the boondocks as Alfred's. She stopped at the end of the driveway and studied the house. Like Alfred's, it was set back from the road, but instead of patchy weeds, the large front lawn was a smooth, green carpet. Flowering bushes flanked the porch where a glider swayed lightly in the breeze. White with green trim, the house appeared to have been recently painted, or at least power-washed. Apple trees filled the fields behind the house.

Marge pulled into the driveway and tugged at her shirt as she stepped out of the car, uncomfortably aware her clothes had already seen her through a long trip from Yakima. She was sure the people who lived in this house would always look presentable—and would never buy their clothes at Wal-Mart.

She closed her eyes for a moment, seeking calm and wisdom, and took a couple of cleansing breaths before approaching the front porch. What exactly did she hope to accomplish here? Well, for one thing, these people were the only ones involved in this tapestry of relationships who were old enough to have understood most of what was going on around them at the time all these boys were born. However, from Carl's reaction, Marge wasn't optimistic about how receptive they would be to telling her what they knew.

After a quick prayer for guidance, she opened her eyes, climbed the stairs to the front door, and knocked. The door opened immediately, as if the woman now facing Marge had been standing behind it waiting for her.

"May I help you?" Mrs. Whiting's voice was cool, uninviting. The rebuff was almost like a slap.

"Hello. My name is Marge Peterson," she managed after an awkward pause. "I'm looking into Alfred Landon's affairs and the death that occurred on his property. I know it might be difficult, but I'd like to talk with you about the things going on in town after your daughter's death."

"I know who you are and why you are in town." Mrs. Whiting didn't move from the doorway. "I don't see how I can help you. I was busy raising my grandson after my daughter died."

Marge noticed she hadn't said her daughter was killed. Perhaps it was too painful to be so blunt. "But surely you heard and saw what was happening around town. From what I've been able to learn, it appears there was some kind of a campaign to smear Alfred Landon's name."

The woman snorted, startling Marge. It was a strange

sound coming from such a refined looking person. "Alfred Landon didn't need any help smearing his name. He did a good job of it all by himself."

"Perhaps, but I have learned he didn't father all those children people assumed he did—possibly none of them. It could be important to discover who actually did."

Mrs. Whiting stared at Marge. "Are you trying to tell me Carl isn't Alfred Landon's son? I wish it were true, but you can't actually believe such a thing."

Marge almost laughed. "No, not Carl, of course. But it is possible Carl and Jerry are the only children he had."

"That's news to me. I wonder why Carl didn't tell me."

"He may not be as convinced of it as I am. After all, he spent his whole life learning to hate the man."

Carl's mother drew herself up tall. "Are you saying I made him hate Alfred Landon?"

"Did you?" Marge could have bitten her tongue. Why did she let things get past her lips before visiting her brain? Confrontation could prevent her from getting any cooperation from this woman.

Mrs. Whiting's eyes narrowed before she sighed and, much to Marge's surprise, backed away from the doorway. "You'd better come in," she said. "I believe we do need to talk. We'll have to do it quickly, though, before my husband gets home."

"I don't like to do anything behind his back, Mrs. Whiting," Marge protested, but she hastened to follow Carl's grandmother into the house.

"My name is Carol. My husband's is Edward. Our daughter's name was Courtney. We never actually adopted Carl but, since Courtney wasn't married to Alfred, Carl is also a Whiting." She paused a moment in the living room, sad eyes sweeping the room.

Marge gazed around. She felt as if she had entered a shrine. The mantel over the large fireplace and every piece of polished cherry furniture were covered with photos of Courtney: baby Courtney laughing in a bubble bath, toddler Courtney in a princess costume, a young Courtney sitting proudly on a horse, teenager Courtney looking radiant in a prom dress, and an array of pictures of Courtney from every school year.

Carol shook her head as if coming to a decision and led Marge into a small sitting room. She gestured for Marge to sit in a cane-backed chair and took the other one herself. This appeared to be Carol Whiting's private room, and in it there was only one small photo of Courtney holding her baby, and one of Carl at his high school graduation.

"Please understand; we had nothing against Alfred before he took up with Courtney." Her voice sounded defensive. "His wife was a wisp of a woman, beautiful but not quite part of this world. After she had Jerry, she seemed even more distant. I have no doubt she died exactly as Alfred said, setting her hut on fire with incense sticks or candles. Alfred doted on her and was never the same after she was gone."

"Do you think grief over Marilyn's death was the reason he started drinking?" Marge asked.

"Yes. He was already a drinker, but he started drinking more heavily after she was gone. Still, it didn't appear to be out of control. He still worked and spent time in town. He was hard on the boy, though. Probably because even though Jerry looked like Alfred, he was a sweet, shy person, a lot like his mother. It might have been too much of a reminder for Alfred."

Marge was emboldened by Carol's candor. "Did you object to Courtney seeing him?"

"I was concerned. We had plans for Courtney. Life here was good for us, with Edward's job at Con Agra; but we thought Courtney would have to leave here to make as good a life for herself. What Alfred would give her was the opposite of everything we wanted for her.

"Her father was livid. Courtney was his little angel and he couldn't fathom how she could be interested in Alfred Landon, a man almost old enough to be her father. He got it into his head that Alfred was somehow forcing her attention." Carol glanced at Marge out of the corner of her eye. "You've seen Carl, so you know what Alfred looked like before the drink got to him. What girl wouldn't have her head turned? I always suspected Courtney threw herself at him, but her father would never believe it.

"Before long, I discovered Courtney was sleeping with Alfred. Since she was going to do what she wanted no matter what I said, I started working to get her on birth control without her father knowing. Before I could accomplish it, she discovered she was pregnant. She was ecstatic. She finally confided in me that Alfred had told her from the beginning he would never marry again, but she thought a baby would change his mind."

"But it didn't?"

"No. She didn't give up hope, though. Once Carl was born she tried to get Alfred to take an interest in him. Alfred didn't. In fact, Alfred refused to see Courtney after he found out she was pregnant. I was glad, because he had started drinking more and I didn't want to put her baby in the same situation we were beginning to see Jerry enduring.

"When Courtney killed herself …" Carol's breath caught for a moment. "When Courtney killed herself, her father refused to believe she would do such a thing. He was convinced Alfred killed her because she turned away his advances. I couldn't raise an objection without causing a storm, so I gave up."

"And the other women who became pregnant, with Alfred the main suspect?"

Carol shook her head. "I truly don't know anything about them. I always suspected he was an easy target for suspicion. After Courtney killed herself, I don't believe he ever took up with another woman. Guilt, I guess."

"Why does Carl believe Alfred fathered all these children?"

"Once the town gossips started spreading the rumors, Edward made sure Carl believed it. Edward always blamed Alfred for the loss of his perfect angel, and he wanted Carl to idolize Courtney and share his hate for Alfred. I wish I had tried to make a difference, but it was too difficult to go against Edward."

The two women had been so engrossed in their conversation they failed to hear the car drive up. The back door slammed open and a large, florid man came charging into the room. His face was so red and his eyes so bulging, Marge feared he might suffer a heart attack.

"What's that woman doing in my house? Why are you talking to her? Carl told me how she's trying to get Alfred off, even though they finally have something to pin on him. Don't you say another word to her." He turned to Marge. "Get out of my house! Get out, right now!"

Marge stood, holding up her hands in surrender as she retreated to the door. "I didn't come to cause any trouble …" she began.

"No trouble?" Edward shouted. "You've been nothing but trouble ever since you stepped foot in this town. Staying in my son's house, no less. You'd better get out of there before he hears about you hassling us."

Marge hurried to her car and sped away as fast as she could without making a mess of the perfect lawn, which she was sure would be the last straw tipping Mr. Whiting into a heart attack.

The man was right about one thing. It would be best if she got out of Carl's house before he came home from work. Ignoring the speed limit, Marge raced to Carl's house. Without even knocking, she ran in and past a startled Angela, and headed straight to the room she had been using. She packed up her belongings as quickly as she could and detoured to the other bedroom to gather anything Eric had left before stopping to explain why she was leaving.

"Since Carl made it clear he didn't want me bothering his grandparents, he is not going to be happy with me," she finished. "And, if he had a thought about being forgiving, his grandfather will make sure he changes his mind."

"Yes, most of the time Carl is his own person and makes his own decisions. He can't seem to do anything against his grandfather's wishes, though. I agree, you had better leave. Where will you go?"

"Back to the motel. Thank you so much for allowing me to stay here."

Angela gave Marge a quick hug. "I'm sure I'll see you again before you go back to Bellevue. And, while I don't think you should continue meddling in our affairs, our connection to Eric makes us family. We want to see more of you both after this is all behind us."

"Absolutely," Marge replied, thinking Angela was as beautiful inside as she was outside. Carl was a lucky man. She hurried out to the car and was a block down the street when she saw Carl's car headed for home. Pretending she didn't see him, she continued on her way.

Marge realized she had probably cut off any possible connection with Carl, at least until after this case was over, and, in consequence, lost her source of any information the police might gather. She wished she knew where Carl was in the process of getting the DNA comparisons. For a moment, she considered asking Angela to get information from Carl for her. The moment passed. It wouldn't be fair to involve Angela in tricking Carl, even if Angela would consider doing it.

Marge didn't quite know how she arrived clear back at the Dusty Café, but she had. She didn't know what to do next. Her mind kept jumping back and forth between remorse at angering Carl and a new sense of urgency about finding Leroy.

It took two cups of coffee and half a bagel before her brain kicked in. Even though she couldn't understand where the urgency about finding Leroy came from, she couldn't wait to finish the bagel before going back to where she had started—the library. She was sure Cynthia would know where Leroy lived and, if she didn't, would know how to find out.

"Hey," Cynthia said as soon as Marge walked in. "What's the story about your little guy? Have they found him?"

Marge blinked. So much had happened in the last

twenty-four hours. She couldn't keep track of who knew what.

"He's fine," Marge said. "In fact, he's with my husband and probably back in Bellevue by now."

"Oh, I'm so glad to hear it," Cynthia said. "He is a real charmer. So, how can I help you today?"

"I need to get in touch with Leroy, the other man people say is Alfred's illegitimate son, but I never got his last name. Do you know what it is?"

"Norland," Cynthia said.

"I can probably find his address in the phone book."

"You don't need a phone book to find Leroy. He isn't from Dusty, he's from Pasco, but Dusty kids go to high school in Pasco. He is still friends with my cousin, who was in his class, and we hang out together every so often." Cynthia took a slip of paper from the desk and wrote down the address. "Why do you want to talk to Leroy? I thought Carl had Alfred all but convicted."

"I'm not a hundred percent certain Alfred did it. We already discovered he wasn't Dan's biological father. If he isn't Leroy's biological father, I wonder who is—and if it is the same person."

"Well, Alfred wasn't the only letch in town," Cynthia said.

Marge stared at her. "Do you have someone else in mind?"

Cynthia looked uncomfortable. "I probably shouldn't say anything, and I'm sure no one else will, but if it really was Brent, the mayor's son, who got Tina pregnant, he learned the art of seduction from an expert."

"His father? If the mayor was also known to sleep

around, why was Alfred blamed for every unexpected pregnancy? Why didn't suspicion ever fall on Brent or the mayor?"

Cynthia shrugged. "I didn't say the mayor fathered those boys," she said. "But if he did, he had the money and the influence to keep anyone from looking too closely at him."

"Maybe I should talk with the mayor," Marge said.

"Too late." Cynthia twisted her fingers together. "His son says he has some kind of dementia and is under medical supervision. Besides, he wasn't the only one. Small towns can be hotbeds of intrigue sometimes."

Marge felt dizzy as she stared at Cynthia. "You know of more illegitimate children?" How many people was she now going to have to investigate?

Cynthia shrugged. "No, I really don't know of any more. All I know is there were a couple of divorces where the children's paternity came into question. But I'm sure suspicious pregnancies happen in every town."

"Thank you for telling me about the mayor, anyway. And for Leroy's address. You've been a great help."

Marge returned to her trusty Honda. She laid her head back against the seat and tried to think. What should she do now? She needed to talk with Carl about all of this, but would he be receptive? There was only one way to find out. She picked up her cell phone and dialed his number.

"Yes, Marge, what can I do for you?" His voice sounded hard, clipped.

"I'm sorry, Carl. I didn't have anyone else to go to who was an adult at the time all this was happening."

"Did my parents shed enough light on this investigation to make it worth upsetting them the way you did?"

"I upset your father," Marge ventured. Obviously Carl considered the couple his parents rather than his grandparents. "Your mother didn't have a problem talking with me."

The line was silent for a moment. "My father was only protecting my mother," he said. "You pushed yourself in to grill my mother and nearly sent my father into another heart attack."

Another? Marge cringed. "I don't want to argue with you about it," she said. "Your mother won't speak against your father; so there is no way I can convince you, but she talked with me freely and willingly. I know you will never forgive me, but can we get past it and talk about the investigation?"

Carl's voice was still cold, but he finally asked, "What do you want to know?"

"Did Leroy bring his DNA results in to be compared with Alfred's?"

"Yes, and he gave a fresh swab, too, to make sure nothing went wrong."

"And he couldn't get his mother to say anything more about his biological father?"

"No, and his legal father won't say if he knows anything, either. Something has everyone refusing to name names."

Marge took a deep breath. "Was the man everyone calls the mayor ever linked to any extramarital activities?"

"What are you getting into now, Marge? There would be no town of Dusty if it weren't for Eugene Martell. I understand his condition is so bad that he is under constant medical supervision. I hope you can leave him in peace."

Marge stared out the windshield at the town the mayor had built before answering. "I'd like to. The man has obviously done a lot of good here. The solution is as simple as getting a DNA sample from him."

"Which his son, as his legal guardian, would have to agree to."

"And why wouldn't his son agree to it?"

"Marge, none of this has any bearing on Alfred killing Dan. The case against him is open and shut. Alfred will never be able to get custody of Eric, so you have no reason to hang around. Please, go back to Bellevue. Let us handle our own affairs."

Marge was about to protest when she realized the line was dead.

Leroy was obviously as interested as Marge was in discovering the identity of his biological father. If he couldn't get his mother to talk, Marge certainly wouldn't be able to. So, was Carl right? Was there nothing left for her to do? Somehow, even though she had no good reason to do so, she knew she had to get in touch with Leroy.

Besides, she still didn't have proof Alfred had killed Dan. She still didn't want Eric to believe his grandfather was a killer if it wasn't true. There must be something more she could do to get at the truth.

Before she could think of any course of action, the shrill of several sirens pierced the air. Looking toward the police station, she saw the two Dusty Township patrol cars race down the street and out of town in the direction of Alfred's place, lights flashing. A moment later, an emergency aid vehicle from the fire station down the block raced past her.

Marge slammed the Honda into gear and took off, following the sirens.

# FIFTEEN

The sirens ended simultaneously, leaving an eerie silence in which Marge's ears kept ringing. The three emergency vehicles surrounded a spot about half a mile past the Landon homestead. Red and blue lights continued to strobe.

Inching the Honda as close as she dared, Marge stepped out and crept toward the center of activity. A red Corvette lay at an impossible angle in a deep culvert on the right side of the road, almost directly across from the two-track where Marge had hidden her car when she went to get Eric. The driver's side was crushed.

The EMTs were working over a man Marge presumed was the driver. She wondered how they had managed to extract him from the wreck. Spotting Carl, she walked toward him. She took a deep breath, hoping he would talk to her.

"Who is it?" she asked quietly as she stepped up beside him.

He gave her a grave look. "Leroy Norland," he said.

Marge's breath came out in a small explosion. "Leroy … really? What a coincidence." After taking a moment to digest the news, she looked around. "No other vehicles?"

"No," Carl said. "The two-track is torn up, as if a car

accelerated quickly, spinning its tires in the dirt. It's pretty obvious someone deliberately slammed into the side of Leroy's car, pushing it off the road. We'll have to wait for the forensics team to complete their investigation, and hope they can find something more."

"But ... Leroy? Now?" Marge exclaimed.

"We won't jump to any conclusions," Carl announced, which made Marge hide a grin. He was all too happy to jump to the conclusion that Alfred killed Dan.

Unable to discover anything more, Marge returned to her car and watched the police continue their investigation. Leroy was loaded onto a gurney and taken away in the emergency vehicle. At least he appeared to be alive. So far.

Breathing a prayer for Leroy, Marge saw new activity at the scene. The county investigators had arrived. Some walked a wide perimeter around the Corvette, taking pictures. Some searched the area and put down little tents indicating evidence of some sort. Some took pictures of the surrounding area. She saw an officer scrape the dented side of the Corvette and put whatever he had scraped off in a small plastic bag. The officer showed the bag to Carl, who proceeded to take his own sample. Carl put his small envelope into a large duffle bag. Marge slipped out of the Honda and wandered as casually as possible toward the scene, but was intercepted before she could discover what had interested the policemen. She guessed it was paint of a different color.

Carl got into his police car and turned back toward town. Marge wanted to find out what they had scraped off Leroy's car, so she ran back to her Honda to follow Carl. She started to accelerate to catch up with him, but had to slow down quickly because, instead of continuing to town, Carl turned in at the Landon driveway.

Why was he going there? She let the Honda creep forward enough so she could watch. She was at the end of the driveway, where she had no cover, so she could only hope Carl wouldn't look back. He strode around Jerry's Impala, inspecting it, before he pulled another small bag out of his pocket, scraped some paint into it, and dropped the evidence bag into the duffle bag. Head down, he turned and walked back to his car. Marge quickly shifted into reverse and drove as far back down the side of the road as she could until she saw the trunk of Carl's car emerge from the driveway. If Carl looked her way he'd still be able to see her, and he'd surely guess she had followed him from the crime scene. She didn't relax her grip on the steering wheel until Carl drove toward town without a glance in her direction.

Marge waited a good five minutes after his car had disappeared from view. Once she was certain he wasn't coming back, she parked near the end of the driveway and walked the rest of the way to Jerry's green car, where she followed Carl's path around it.

"Oh, no," she whispered. The right front corner of the car was bashed in and the headlight was broken. Bending down to look closer, Marge put her hand on the hood to steady herself. She stood, startled. The hood was warm. The car had been recently driven. And, in the area where she had seen Carl scrape off some paint, Marge saw why he had done it. Embedded in the gouges on the green paint were traces of red.

She stepped back, puzzled. Why would Jerry ram Leroy's car, forcing it off the road, and leave the scene only to park his battered car in his own driveway without any attempt to hide the evidence? Was it possible Jerry was drunk and drove into Leroy without realizing what he had done, and then driven the rest of the way home and parked the car as usual? She shook her head. If Jerry was that drunk, how could he have maneuvered his car away from the crash site?

Marge was certain that whoever hit Leroy had done it on purpose. Why else would they come hurtling out of the two-track, tearing up the dirt, and hit Leroy almost broadside?

And, of course, there would be no witnesses. Traffic was practically nonexistent out here, heading away from town up a dirt road that seemed to go nowhere. Leroy must have had a reason to be on the road, though. Who would have known he'd be here?

The damage to Jerry's car was only on the front bumper of the passenger side, indicating Leroy was a little past the two-track before the collision. Whoever was driving the Impala would have had to back off after the collision and turn in this direction to get the car into Jerry's driveway. Marge looked around, but couldn't see any tire tracks on the packed-down dirt. Assuming Jerry wasn't the driver, where had the person gone after parking the Impala? Marge peered into the car. She blinked. The keys were in the ignition!

Marge heard a car pull in the driveway behind her. She froze. At the same moment she heard a car door open, Jerry emerged from the house rubbing his eyes. He was dressed in rumpled clothes that looked as if they had been slept in.

*"What are you doing here?!"*

Marge swiveled her head, unnerved by the question barked at her in stereo from two directions.

"Snooping?" she answered without thinking.

"Don't you think it's about time you stopped?" Carl asked from behind her.

"What are you snooping at?" Jerry asked. He looked groggy as he staggered down the steps and out to his car. "Hey!" he hollered. "What the hell happened to my car?"

"Suppose you tell me," Carl replied.

"It was fine when I drove it last night," Jerry said. "I conked out early, about nine—didn't wake up until a few minutes ago. Slept like I was drugged or something."

"Yeah, right," Carl said. "So someone else took your car and forced Leroy off the road, and then drove it back here?"

"Could've happened," Jerry muttered. He stopped, frowned, and scratched his head. "Wait! Someone ran Leroy off the road?"

Marge studied Jerry. Unfortunately, his obvious puzzlement would mean nothing to anyone who thought he had been too drunk to remember the accident.

"Carl, would it hurt to look around to see if there are any signs of someone being on the property recently?" asked Marge.

"In addition to you and me and all those officers who traipsed around in here to search for Eric?" Carl asked, his voice caustic.

Marge nodded. "You have a point. But, the hood of Jerry's car is still warm; someone might have been here minutes before you arrived today. There might be some fresh evidence."

Carl was shaking his head.

Marge hurried on, before he could shut her off. "Also, can you have Jerry's blood tested, in case he was drugged and there is something still in his system?"

"What would finding drugs in his system prove? As much as he drinks, he might do drugs, too."

"Can Jerry ask to have his blood tested?" Marge asked.

Carl frowned. "He's going into custody now, for vehicular assault; which will be upgraded to manslaughter or murder if Leroy dies. By the time the county guys get him to Pasco and get him processed, if he has any drug in his system now, it will be long gone."

Marge stared at Carl as he cuffed Jerry and led him to the police car. He was doing it again. He jumped to the conclusion Jerry did it and wouldn't even consider any other possibility. Why was Carl so eager to get Alfred and Jerry out of the way? If Dan and Leroy were both dead, and Jerry and Alfred were in prison, Carl would be the only one left to inherit whatever Alfred had to give. What *did* he have? Had there been a large life insurance policy on Marilyn after all?

No, not only Carl. There was also Eric. She was suddenly very glad Eric was in Bellevue with Pete.

"Wait a minute," she called. "How bad is Leroy hurt?"

Carl didn't show any sign of answering her.

"Didn't Alfred say there was no insurance money?" Marge pursued. "And didn't Jerry say he knew Leroy wasn't Alfred's son? Why would Jerry try to kill Leroy?"

Carl slammed the door behind Jerry and turned to face Marge. His face was dark and scowling. "You are so ready to believe these drunks," he said. "Jerry said what he knew would be in his best interests. Alfred did the same. Stop trying to make them into something they're not."

He was halfway into the driver's seat before he added, "You need to leave this yard now and not go anywhere near Jerry's car. Enough evidence has already been compromised."

Marge stared after him as he drove away. Was it possible Carl was the one twisting everything to be in his own best interests? If Carl could get rid of "these drunks," maybe he could forget they were his relatives. Feeling as though she had hit rock bottom, she trudged down the driveway to her car and drove slowly back to town.

Even if Leroy wasn't badly hurt, there was no way Marge would be able to talk with him for a day or two. She didn't have a day or two. Did she have to start ruling out possible fathers for Leroy and Dan one man at a time from the entire male population of Dusty? That would be impossible.

But, she thought, her mind shifting into gear and her foot pressing harder on the gas pedal, she could start with the one who had already been called to her attention—the man they called "the mayor." How hard would it be to get a sample of his DNA for testing? Did Cynthia say he was under medical care? If he was in a nursing home, could Marge find out which one?

The police couldn't get a DNA sample without permission or a court order, but maybe Marge could. If she could get a sample from the mayor, maybe she could have it compared to Leroy's DNA results. Did you need any proof of permission from the donor in order to get a DNA test done?

Marge pulled up in front of the library. This was becoming like her second home. Cynthia looked up from her desk, a worried look furrowing her brows.

"Any word about Leroy?" she asked.

"News travels fast," Marge said. "No, I don't think we'll hear anything for a while." She paused. "Do you know what nursing home the man you called the mayor is in?"

"Why?"

"I'm grasping at straws now, but what if the mayor is Dan and Leroy's biological father? If so, we're looking in the wrong direction to discover who would want them out of the picture."

Cynthia looked thoughtful. "This could explain why Brent is in town so much all of a sudden."

"Brent, the mayor's son?"

"Yes, Brent Martell. The mayor's name is Eugene Martell. He has an estate not far from the Whitings. It's probably been sitting empty for a while, at least as much as anyone knows. Rumor is Brent put Eugene in a nursing home. Brent always acted as if he's a big fish like his daddy, but it appeared this pond was too small for him. I always thought *Daddy* wouldn't continue to underwrite Brent's lifestyle if Brent didn't stay home, but he spends a lot of time in Portland and at the casinos and, as far as anyone knows, the mayor still supports him.

"I've seen Brent drive through town a couple of times in the last week, which is unusual. I wondered if he was taking charge since Eugene is incapacitated. I expect we'll have the answer soon if he puts their house on the market, although I don't know if he could find anyone rich enough to buy it who would want to live out in the boondocks."

"Is Brent a big gambler?"

Cynthia shrugged. "Not enough to cause any problems, as far as I know, but I don't suppose either he or the mayor would let it become public knowledge if he was. He used to run over to the Wild Horse Casino in Pendleton when-ever he could, but mostly I thought it was because he could party there. They do manage to keep their personal lives pretty private for a small town."

"Do you know where Eugene Martell is now?"

"No." She picked up her phone and dialed a number. "Elsie? This is Cynthia. Could you tell me where Eugene Martell's mail is being forwarded? What? No, he has some overdue books and I'd like to see if I can get them back. Well, thank you, anyway."

Marge stared at her. "Was that legal?"

Cynthia grinned. "We bend the rules sometimes. It doesn't help you, though, because his mail isn't being for-warded. Evidently Brent picks it up at the house."

"I need to talk with Brent. Where is this palace?"

"About a mile past the Whiting house," Cynthia said, straightening her desk and stacking books on the return cart. She laughed at Marge's look of surprise. "It's well past closing time. I forgot to lock the door before settling down to do some paperwork or you would never have caught me."

"Where has the day gone?" Marge asked. "I'd better get myself into my motel. Could I buy you dinner?"

Cynthia shook her head. "Family conference tonight. My husband and I make our two teenagers join us once a week to find out what is happening in each other's lives and hope we can trust them to be honest with us."

~

Marge had already reserved her room at the motel in Pasco. She bought a bottle of Merlot at the general store and put them it in her car before stopping at the Dusty Café for a bite to eat. As soon as she entered, aromas of garlic and basil washed over her. The healthy salad she had been planning on eating didn't seem appealing any more. She opted for the special of the day: herb-crusted trout and garlic roasted potatoes with green beans amandine.

Five minutes after Marge placed her order, the door opened. Out of curiosity she glanced up. The man who strode in looked familiar. Had she seen him before? Where? She studied him as he paid for a large takeout package and left without greeting anyone—unusual in this small town.

Marge shook her head. She couldn't put her finger on what made her feel as if she recognized him.

"What do you think that wastrel is doing back in town?" she heard at the next table.

"Probably looking for whatever else he can get off his father. Guess it serves the old goat right for catering to him all his life."

"Can you believe he stopped in here for takeout? Couldn't lower himself to eat with the masses, but evidently doesn't have a cook at the manor anymore."

Marge's ears perked up. Now she had an idea who they were talking about.

"Well, I don't think he's alone. Did you see the size of the takeout? It looked like enough for three. I wonder what unlucky woman is trying to capture him now. At least she'll get a decent meal out of her troubles!"

The server arrived with Marge's bread and salad, causing her to miss the next bits of conversation.

"… heard the old man doesn't have a mind left. He must

have given Brent power of attorney. Bet the kid stuck him in a nursing home and forgot all about him."

"Guess his high-powered attorney wasn't worth all that much. You'd think the old man would have made sure he was well taken care of in his old age."

The server came to their table with the bill.

"Honey, we forgot to tell you, separate bills. Can you do that now?"

"No problem," the weary woman answered, taking back the bill.

"You'd think they'd ask."

"Hey, go easy. I went to school with Evelyn, and she has enough on her plate."

Marge's dinner arrived and she bowed her head in silent prayer. She thanked God she didn't have to be on her feet all day serving ungrateful customers. It could have happened. She also thanked God for what she had overheard. On top of what Cynthia had told her, this added a new angle to her investigation. She prayed for strength and wisdom to do what needed to be done to get to the truth.

Raising her head, she dug into her wonderfully aromatic plate of food. She felt rejuvenated. She had a new lead to follow tomorrow. Maybe it would put her on the path to solving this case and heading back to Bellevue.

~

Her euphoria lasted until she returned to her motel room and called Pete.

"Ben's not home yet," Pete said.

"Did he come home last night?"

"Yes, Olivia waited up for him. But he was gone again this morning, with his usual stash of food, before she awoke."

"I should be there," Marge said, shaking her head. "What was I thinking?"

"There is nothing you could do if you were here. I'd like you home as soon as possible, but you were right to go back. If you leave there now and we never clear things up about Eric's grandfather, you'll always blame yourself."

After their conversation, Marge collapsed into bed, but she knew it was only to begin a night of tossing and turning.

"Please, God," she prayed aloud. "Take care of my Benjamin. Don't let anyone hurt him."

# SIXTEEN

Pete rubbed his hands over the rough stubble on his face. He knew Marge felt she had to finish what she was doing, but knowing how she felt didn't make it any easier to stay on top of Ben's actions without her help. It wasn't as if he could ask the department for manpower to search for an addict who had escaped from enforced rehab. Nor could the department spare manpower to look for Ben again, after he somehow shook their tail and made his way to his mother in Seattle.

Olivia and Robert gave Pete all the time they could spare, but they had their own jobs. Pete was using vacation time so he would be available 24/7 in case Ben decided to trust him to help with his mother. So far, it didn't look as though he would.

Pete was about ready to phone his mother to ask her to come over and stay with Eric while he went out looking for Ben when Ben crept in the kitchen door.

Pete's frustration made him flare up in anger. "You're pushing your time limits, Ben!" he barked.

Ben frowned and slouched, his hands stuffed in his pockets.

Pete could have bitten his tongue. It wouldn't help if he drove the boy away.

Eric came rushing out of his bedroom. "You found your mother!" he exclaimed. "Is she all right?"

Eric's question felt like a slap in the face to Pete. It was the kind of question he should be asking—should have already asked.

Ben straightened up at the sight of Eric, sporting the first smile Pete had seen on his face in days. "When did you get home?" he asked. The smile disappeared as quickly as it had come. Ben snapped his mouth shut and glared at Pete, his frown back in place.

Something about Ben looked different. It took Pete a moment to realize what it was. Ben did not have the bag he was using to carry food to his mother.

"Didn't you and your mother eat all the food today?" Pete asked, thinking maybe Ben left the bag with food in it for his mother to finish.

Ben stood on one foot, then the other, staring at the floor.

What was he hiding? And why? Pete had made it clear to Ben that it was okay if he took food. Something was definitely wrong.

"What did you do with the food today, Ben?" he ventured.

"Gave it away."

The answer came so quickly it was obvious Ben had rehearsed it, but his voice was so low Pete could barely hear him.

"Who did you give it to?" Pete pushed.

"Somebody on the street." Ben spoke a little louder this time, sounding defensive.

"You didn't give it to your mother?" Pete asked in as gentle a voice as he could manage.

Ben didn't answer. He shoved his fists deeper into his pockets and continued to stare at the floor.

"Is your mother still hungry, Ben? Did you have to give the food to someone else?" Pete asked.

When Ben finally looked up, Pete saw tears in the corners of his eyes. "Ben, you can't leave your mother hungry out there. You know what she will do to get food. And she will be right back where she was before. Let us help her."

Ben's head came up, his blue eyes hard. "She ain't using. It'd kill her to be locked up again."

Pete shook his head. Ben was avoiding the issue of his mother hooking for food and money. Pete wouldn't force it right now. "No, she'll only feel miserable for a while—until she is truly clean and the poison is out of her system. It would be the best thing you could do for her..."

"No!" Ben shouted. "You don't know her. You don't know what she needs. You leave her alone." He stormed into his bedroom and slammed the door.

Ben had a hard time lying. Pete knew Ben was afraid Pete would get his mother's location out of him if he continued to talk. Which Pete wanted to do. Needed to do. But how was he going to do it without alienating the boy for good?

~

Eric still stood in the kitchen, staring after Ben.

"What do you think, pal?" Pete asked. "What can we do to help him?"

Eric shook his head. "Benji don't want help," he said. "Maybe you can let him figure it out for himself."

119

"I wish I could. But even if I could leave his mother out there, I can't let Ben put himself in harm's way to help her. You know the kind of people who have been taking advantage of her. Ben is not safe with them. And if she doesn't go looking for them, you can bet they will come looking for her."

Pete could see the struggle going on behind Eric's hazel eyes. Eric's first loyalty would be to Ben. He would only help Pete if he could be convinced it was in Ben's best interests.

Eric shrugged. "Don't know what I can do," he mumbled before disappearing behind Ben's bedroom door.

Pete stared at the closed door, shattered at feeling rejected by these two boys he had come to consider his sons. He shook himself. That was what happened to parents. But parents were the adults. They had to rise above the pain and disappointment and do what was best for their children.

Right now, he guessed that might be food. Ben looked as though he was starving, and Eric was always hungry. Pete put on one of Marge's aprons and began to prepare spaghetti with meat sauce—food that was sure to bring them out of the bedroom.

# SEVENTEEN

Marge dragged herself out of bed at seven o'clock Friday morning, another sunny day. It was hard to believe this was the same state she lived in. Around Seattle, three days without rain was cause for celebration. Here, she would welcome a little of western Washington's moisture to freshen the breeze.

Her eyes felt gritty from lack of sleep but she was eager to start the new line of investigation, hoping it would lead to some answers so she could finish up and head home.

By the time she had showered and eaten a banana and hard-boiled egg in the motel's café, to make up for last night's gluttony, the sun had already been up two hours.

She clambered gingerly into the old Honda wagon and rolled down the windows. The interior of the car was a good ten degrees hotter than the outside temperature, which was well on its way to the ninety degrees forecast for the day.

Marge lightly tapped the steering wheel, wondering how long it would take to be cool enough to grip, while she tried to think of a way to get into the Martell mansion. Her mind felt as dry as the breeze wafting through the windows. Finally, she grabbed some tissues to hold against the steering wheel, started the car, and headed out of Pasco. She'd have to think of something on the way to Dusty.

By the time she neared the Whiting house, she hadn't succeeded in thinking of anything yet. The immaculate lawn and flower beds and fresh paint on the house made it stand out in glaring contrast to the neighborhood. The elderly couple was busy in their yard; he was riding a power mower across the large expanse of grass and she was pulling weeds from around the flowering shrubs. They hadn't wanted their daughter, Courtney, to spend her life in Dusty, but this is where they raised her; and they looked as if they were here to stay. Could they not bear to leave the only place where they would have memories of their daughter? Or, more likely, they did not want to be separated from their grandson, Carl.

As the mayor's house came into view, Marge had to stop the car and get out for a better look. *Mansion* wasn't the right word. While it appeared spacious, the house was smaller than the Whitings'. It had two stories, but was a modern, compact, stone-and-glass building with solar panels on the roof and two windmills in the back. And either Eugene or Brent Martell must be an auto buff because the house had an attached two-car garage plus a detached garage with three doors.

Although the lawn was lush and green, indicating an underground irrigation system, the grass was in need of mowing and a scattering of dandelions poked their yellow heads up. Dead blossoms hung on the flowering shrubs. Evidently Brent was neglecting the regular outdoor maintenance.

As Marge walked up the driveway, she saw an old, beat-up car parked in front of the house. Was it Brent's? She couldn't picture Brent driving anything so disreputable looking. Besides, wouldn't he put his car in one of the garages?

Looking up, she discovered she had been seen. A white-haired man stood at a window on the second floor, his hand up as if waving. A moment later, he disappeared and the blinds were lowered.

Marge's mind whirled. Was it Eugene Martell? Maybe he wasn't in a nursing home after all. Was the wave meant to get her attention? If so, what could she do about it?

The condition of the yard gave her an idea. She didn't know how far it would get her, but she had to try. Climbing back into the Honda, she drove up the driveway and parked behind the other car. She strode to the front door.

She almost faltered at the appearance of the man who answered the doorbell. "Sir," she said before he could send her away, "I couldn't help notice how beautiful your grounds are, but they are in need of some grooming. The Franklin County Landscaping Service would appreciate an opportunity to explain how we can help you."

She crossed her fingers behind her back and threw up a prayer for forgiveness for the lie, all the while hoping there wasn't a real Franklin County Landscaping Service.

"Go away. We don't need no services."

The door slammed in her face. Marge frowned. Who was that man? Certainly not Brent Martell. With his unkempt hair and scruffy beard, he looked like a thug. Would Brent or his father have hired a caretaker for the property? If so, he wasn't doing a very good job. If Mr. Martell had lost his ability to handle his affairs, it would be Brent who did any hiring. Was the man taking care of Eugene Martell and the property?

Marge backed slowly toward her car, scrutinizing the house as if to find an answer to her dilemma. If she left with nothing, where could she go next? Would Mr. Martell's attorney or doctor know anything about his possible connection with Dan and Leroy? If they did, would they share it with her?

She reached her car and looked up at the second-story window. The shade had been raised again, and the white-haired man's face peered out at her. Once again, he appeared to be waving his hand as if trying to tell her something; then he abruptly looked over his shoulder and disappeared. A moment later, the man who had met her at the front door glared out at her.

Marge frowned. She was now certain Eugene Martell was at home, not in a nursing home. And she suspected the fearsome-looking man might be more than a care-taker. Was Eugene being kept against his will? Maybe the man was guarding Eugene. Did Eugene have some kind of dementia, making a caretaker/guard necessary to keep him safe?

She drove away before the thug would think the old man had succeeded in communicating with her—if that is what he had been trying to do.

She should probably let Carl know what she had seen, if only to make sure he was working with accurate informa-tion. Pulling off the road, she dialed his number on her cell phone. Her call went to voicemail. She wondered if Carl wasn't able to answer his phone or if he had stopped taking calls from her.

She left a message. "Carl, I drove out to the Martell house and discovered Eugene Martell is there—and might be being kept there against his will. Do you know, or can you find out, the name of his doctor or lawyer?"

She hung up, not knowing what else to say. If she were the police, she wouldn't need the doctor or lawyer. She was sure they could find some excuse to insist on talking to Eugene. But she wasn't the police, so she had to find another way in.

Back on the road, the Honda seemed to find its own way to the library. Marge charged in, hardly saying hello to Cynthia, before she sat down at the computer. Her fingers froze on the keys. What was she looking for?

"Can I help?" Cynthia asked.

Marge put her hands in her lap and sighed. "I don't know. I need to find out what Eugene Martell's status is right now. I believe he's in his own house, perhaps being held against his will. I left a message for Carl, but I don't know if the police will believe me or do anything. I thought if I could find Eugene's doctor or his attorney, I might be able to get some information from them, but I don't know where to start. If Eugene made his millions at Microsoft, he probably lived around Bellevue, and he might still have his attorney there. It's a little far to go for a doctor, though."

"All right," Cynthia said. "Assuming the police don't believe you, we can at least prove he's not in a nursing home—if he's not, of course. I'll call every nursing home, starting with the closest and going out about three hundred miles, making sure to include Bellevue. I'll ask for Mr. Martell's room number so I can send him flowers. If he's not there, most of them will tell me without even thinking about it. We'll still have to figure out how to check the places where they won't tell me, but we will have narrowed down the number of nursing homes. Why are we doing this?"

Marge laughed. How fortunate she had been to find an ally who would follow her whims, even if neither of them had any idea what they were doing. "I'm not sure if we need to look into his status, but since Eugene might have some connection to the things going on in Dusty, I think we should check it out. Good idea about calling the nursing homes, since it's possible I'm wrong about who I saw in the house. I'll start with law offices. They also might tell me if he isn't a client, even though they probably would not be able to divulge any information if he is."

Marge and Cynthia went to their separate computers and pulled out their cell phones. Cynthia started going at a fast clip, the nursing homes readily telling her they had no one by the name Martell registered with them. Marge's calls were slower going.

"It doesn't invade anyone's privacy if you tell me whether or not Eugene Martell is a client of your firm," she said over and over. She didn't know if her claim was strictly true, but after she'd said it enough times she found herself believing it.

Marge's calls took longer than Cynthia's but eventually, after she stressed that if he wasn't a client it wouldn't hurt if they said as much, Marge was told Eugene wasn't a client. Marge could only hope the receptionists weren't lying in order to get rid of her.

"How many law firms can counties the size of Franklin and Benton have?" Marge asked, punching in what felt like the hundredth phone number. "I started with Pasco, because it's the closest city. I guess I should try Prosser next, since it's the Franklin County seat."

On her third call to Prosser, panic made Marge sit up straight. They hadn't planned far enough ahead. Holding up her hand to get Cynthia's attention, she said in a loud whisper, "I think I'm being transferred to his attorney! What do I do now?"

Cynthia's eyes widened but the attorney came on the line before Marge could get any words of wisdom from her.

"This is Ron Leonard," he said. "I understand you have some information about Eugene Martell?"

Marge frowned. "You're his attorney?"

"Yes. And you are … ?"

"My name is Marge Peterson."

"All right, Mrs. Peterson. What can you tell me about Eugene?"

"Umm, I was hoping maybe you could tell me something. Have you lost track of him?"

The line was silent. When the attorney spoke again, his voice was dismissive. "I'm afraid I can't say anything more about a client."

"Let me tell you this," Marge hurried to say before he could hang up. "I went out to his house today, to talk with his son. Brent wasn't there. Some other man answered the door and sent me packing, but as I was arriving and again as I was leaving I saw a man in an upstairs window who seemed to be trying to get my attention."

"What did the man look like?"

"It was difficult to see through the window, the way the sun was shining, but I'd say he was an older man, white hair I think, and carrying a little weight."

"You could be describing Eugene Martell," the attorney said. "Exactly what is your interest in him?"

Marge thought a moment. "I'm not sure I have one. You must have heard about the murder at Alfred Landon's farm, near Dusty. Yesterday a car was run off the road, which may well have been another attempted murder. Alfred Landon and his son have been arrested for the two incidents. Both of the young men involved have been suspected of being Alfred's illegitimate sons. Alfred denies he is their father. While looking into the background of these people, Eugene and Brent Martell's names came up. I don't know if they are connected, but I need to find out."

"Why?"

"Alfred Landon is the grandfather of my foster son, who I hope to adopt. I don't want the boy to believe his grandfather is a murderer unless it is true. I have to know."

"I see. Based on what you've told me, I'm going out to the Martell home and try to establish whether Eugene is there and, if so, whether he wishes to talk with you. I don't know if whatever he might tell you will help you with your investigation, but it could prevent you from wasting your time on the wrong premise. Would you give me a number where I can reach you?"

Marge gave him her cell phone number. "Thank you so much, Mr. Leonard. I'll be waiting to hear from you. Could you also inform Carl Whiting, in Dusty, about any concerns you might have? He is investigating the cases."

"I'm afraid Carl Whiting has no legal standing in Franklin County."

"What?" Marge almost barked. "I thought he was a law enforcement officer."

"I guess I can tell you, since it is no secret in town. Eugene came to Dusty with his Microsoft millions and set about creating a kingdom out of what had nearly become a ghost town. One of the first things he did was hire his own law enforcement. Eugene is a large benefactor of county programs, which helped county officials turn a blind eye to what was happening in Dusty; and they even work with Carl as if he were a real deputy since it lightens their load. But Carl is, in reality, a glorified security guard and has no official recognition as a law enforcement officer."

Marge had difficulty breathing. Carl had taken charge of everything, cutting Marge out anytime he wanted—but he had no more legal authority than she did. Well, almost no more legal authority. Obviously, the county police treated him like an honorary deputy or he wouldn't be able to get away with it.

She took a deep breath. "Mr. Leonard, I don't know how to proceed. The town believes Eugene Martell is in a nursing home, too ill to tend to his affairs. His son, Brent, is suddenly about town frequently but has no interaction with anyone here. I saw someone who I believed was Mr. Martell in the window of his house and the person I saw seemed to be asking for help. I've left word with Carl, and now I've told you. Is there anything else I can do?"

"Sit tight and wait to hear from me before you do anything. Once I have determined what the situation is, I'll take any action needed with the proper authorities. I think you can leave it to them to handle."

Cynthia stared at Marge, eyes wide. "I can't believe it," she said. "Mr. Martell has been at his own house all this time? And Brent might be keeping him captive? I wonder why. I know Mr. Martell is terminally ill—one of the nurses at the hospital is not as discreet as she ought to be, so the whole town knows. If he is terminally ill, why would Brent keep him captive?"

Why, indeed? Marge thought. If her suspicions were correct, all these events were connected to something Brent wanted. What more than Eugene Martell's huge estate could he possibly want?

# EIGHTEEN

~~~~~~~~

Marge crossed the street to the café and ordered an iced coffee and an egg salad sandwich. While waiting for her lunch, she pulled out her sketch pad and drew as good a likeness of Eugene Martell as she could remember. As usual, her fingers made the image clearer than the one in her memory. Marge frowned. Something about it was familiar.

She turned the page back to the sketch of Dan and stared. Yes, it was certainly possible. She closed her eyes to bring back the image of the man who had picked up takeout at the café last night. She drew his face quickly. It looked remarkably like the man she saw in the window. Without a doubt, the man in the window was Brent's father. There was an echo of their striking similarity in Dan's face, also. She couldn't be certain, and she had to admit her predisposition to believe there was a connection might have influenced her sketches, but from what she had drawn, she was fairly certain Eugene Martell was Dan's biological father.

What about Leroy?

Pulling out her cell phone, she called Carl.

"What now, Marge?" was Carl's grumpy greeting.

"Would you tell me what hospital Leroy was taken to?"

The line was silent for a moment. "Well, it will take

you about five minutes to discover the nearest hospital is Lourdes Medical Center in Pasco. I doubt you can get in to see him, though."

She didn't want to debate the issue with him, and she had the information she needed. "Did you get my message about seeing Mr. Martell at his house?" she asked, hoping to divert his attention.

"Yes, and I called the house to see what was going on. The gentleman who answered was a healthcare worker Brent hired so he could bring his father home."

"He didn't look much like a healthcare worker to me!"

"And, what *exactly* does a healthcare worker look like?" Carl's voice was caustic.

Marge swallowed. The man had looked like a thug, and the way he treated her seemed more like the actions of a thug than a healthcare worker. But how could she convince Carl or anyone else?

As soon as she disconnected with Carl, she would draw a sketch of the man in case she ever had to try to make her point. In the meantime, she decided to not say anything about Ron Leonard going out to the house. It would be better if she didn't appear connected to the attorney's actions.

"Has the county taken Jerry into custody yet?" she asked as another diversionary tactic.

"Yes, they took him in last night."

"Were you able to test Jerry for drugs?"

"We really don't have the facilities here to test for drugs, Marge. Besides, as I told you before, he most likely did have drugs as well as alcohol in his system, so it would prove nothing."

Frustration made Marge say more than she intended. "Jerry's description of what happened to him sounds remarkably like what happened to Alfred. If you discovered some kind of knock-out drug in his system, it might indicate he was innocent. I'm beginning to believe you want those two men put away where you don't have to deal with the reality of your relationship anymore."

"I think we're finished here, Marge," Carl said, his voice decidedly cold. The line went dead.

Gulping the last of her iced coffee, Marge sidled up to the bar to catch the waitress' attention.

"Was it my imagination, or did the man who picked up a large takeout dinner last night not pay for it?" she asked.

The waitress laughed. "Brent never pays. We keep tabs on him, though, and his father always paid the bill when we did the books at the end of the month." She frowned. "Mr. Martell is ill, so he hasn't been around for a couple months. We don't know what is going to happen in the future."

Marge's head spun at this new information. "Why would Mr. Martell be going over the books with you?"

"Oh, the café belongs to him. He never interfered with our running it, especially after he taught us how to make sure the books balanced."

Did this whole town belong to Eugene Martell? Was Carl trying to avoid a confrontation with him and Brent to protect his position? If so, would Dusty turn back into a ghost town after Eugene died, or would Brent suddenly take an interest once he became the power on the throne?

She shook her head to stop the onslaught of speculation. "Do you know the address of Lourdes Medical Center?" she asked the waitress.

The woman tore off a cash receipt and wrote the address. She looked up as she handed it to Marge, tears glistened in her eyes. "Are you going to see Leroy? Be sure to tell him all his old friends here in Dusty are praying for him."

Marge glanced back at Dusty in the rearview mirror as she drove out of town. She found herself praying the town would survive the death of its benefactor. Whatever his motivation in creating his own little fiefdom, it had become a community quite a few people were happy to call home.

As the back-country roads gave way to paved highways, Marge tried to think of a way to get a look at Leroy. If he was still in ICU, probably only family members would be allowed in his room, and she was sure he would have enough family members there to make it impossible for Marge to fake being one.

She was right. Leroy's wife and mother were both at the hospital. His mother's eyes were glazed. "Leroy's condition has stabilized enough for him to be moved from intensive care to a hospital room," she said in a monotone. "But he still hasn't regained consciousness."

"What was he doing out there, anyway?" Her voice high-pitched and thin, Leroy's wife sounded as if the question had been repeating itself over and over in her head. For some reason, she seemed to expect an answer from Marge. When she didn't get one, she ranted on, "He never had any reason to go to Dusty, let alone out on that side of town. The only things out there are vineyards and large farms affiliated with firms like Del Monte and Con Agra. Leroy is a computer programmer for the city of Pasco. He didn't have any business out there. I don't understand it."

Leroy's mother put an arm around her daughter-in-law's

shoulder to calm her. The glazed look had gone from her eyes. She narrowed them at Marge, as if seeing her for the first time. "I'm sorry, but who are you? What do you have to do with Leroy? Why are you here?" She fired off the questions in rapid succession.

Marge thought fast. She knew she didn't have any business here, and it was hardly the time to ask who Leroy's father might be.

"I want to help find out what happened to both Dan and Leroy," she managed.

"Well, please leave. We don't need anything more to upset Lyla; and we have no idea what happened," she said.

"I will," Marge promised. "May I take a peek in the room and give Leroy greetings from his friends in Dusty?"

"What friends in Dusty?" his wife almost wailed. "He didn't have anything to do with Dusty."

"High school," Leroy's mother said, squeezing her shoulder. "You know, Dusty kids were bused to Pasco for high school. They had reunions and stayed in touch. Calm down, Lyla." She looked hard at Marge. "If we allow you to talk to him, will you leave us alone?"

"Yes," Marge promised.

"All right. I'll give you a moment and no more."

Marge stepped through the door, which closed behind her. She zeroed in on Leroy's face, committing it to memory. He looked peaceful, as if he were in a deep sleep, but Marge knew people in a coma were often able to hear what was going on around them. "Everyone in Dusty is worried and praying for you," she said. She put her hand lightly on his arm. "And I am praying you will feel God's presence as he helps you through whatever is in store."

The door swung open, making Marge jump. The woman was serious when she said only a moment. "Now leave," Leroy's mother said in a loud whisper.

Marge did. As soon as she got to the Honda she whipped out her drawing pad and sketched a likeness of Leroy.

"Yes," she said aloud, when she compared it with the other sketches. She had little doubt the three men were related. Her jubilation subsided. "So, what difference does it make if they are related?"

Even if Dan and Leroy are Eugene's biological sons, why was someone trying to get rid of them? No one suspected the relationship, and Eugene had never admitted parentage. If he was their father, he had taken strong measures to ensure it was kept secret. Had something happened to change his mind and he was now ready to recognize and provide for them?

Brent was his father's only legitimate son; he probably had nothing to fear from them even if he had somehow discovered they were his half-brothers. The only catch would be if Dan or Leroy somehow found out and decided to sue for their portion of the inheritance. Although, it didn't appear they *had* found out.

It seemed as if everyone believed whoever was trying to kill Dan and Leroy thought they were Alfred Landon's sons. They weren't; and no one had come up with a reason someone would kill them because Alfred was their father, anyway.

None of which automatically meant they were Eugene Martell's sons either. Only Marge's gut, and her fingers, were convinced of that.

# NINETEEN

~~~~~~~~~~

Marge felt drained. Since she was already in Pasco, she decided to return to her motel room. Relaxing for a few minutes might help get her thoughts in order.

As she lay on the bed, she knew she had to finish here soon. She had already been here four nights. The motel was costing her money, she had work piling up at the framing shop back home, and she needed to help Benjamin sort out his relationship with his mother. A yearning for Pete and the boys brought her close to tears.

Her cell phone rang, startling Marge from her reverie. She picked it up quickly, her heart thumping at what she might hear. Had Benjamin come home last night? Had he decided to stay with his mother?

"I'm sorry I didn't call sooner," Pete said. "Ben did come home last night. He has been taking food to his mother in a tote bag, but he didn't have the bag with him last night. He became even more upset than usual when I tried to talk about it. I got the feeling the food was taken from him, so neither he nor his mother got any of it. I made spaghetti for the boys and he ate as if he hadn't had anything to eat all day, which I believe might be the case."

"Has he gone back out today?" Marge asked.

"Yes, he was gone before I awoke again. He took another

tote bag full of food. I don't know what more I can do. I can't tie him down."

"We'll have to pray for wisdom," Marge said with a sigh. Could she solve this thing for Eric so she could head home by tomorrow afternoon?

Sitting at the motel room desk after ending her conversation with Pete, Marge ripped a fresh sheet of paper from her drawing pad. After scratching her head for a moment, she began writing down the names of all the people who might have been involved in Dan's murder and the assault on Leroy.

For Dan's murder, Alfred was on the scene, too drunk to know whether or not he had shot the gun. He could only keep repeating that Dan was not his son.

Jerry, Alfred's only legitimate son, left Bellevue early enough to have arrived at his father's house before the murder happened.

Carl Whiting, also Alfred's son, might have wanted to get rid of a potential heir to Alfred's estate by killing Dan.

Brent Martell had the same motive as Carl, if he believed Dan was actually *his* father's biological son, and not Alfred's.

Had either Carl or Brent figured out Dan wasn't Alfred's biological son?

Marge supposed Leroy, Alfred's other alleged son, should also be included as a suspect, but she wasn't sure why except for the double connection with Dan—first, believing he and Dan were both Alfred's offspring; and, secondly, possibly discovering they were biological brothers but with a different shared father.

According to Dan's mother, after learning Alfred wasn't

his biological father, Dan felt obligated to apologize to Alfred for the discomfort the false claim had cost him.

Since Alfred knew Dan wasn't his son, what reason would he have for shooting Dan? It seemed all too easy and coincidental to say Alfred was drunk and mistook Dan for a trespasser. Plus, if Alfred was that drunk, would he have been able to hold the shotgun steady enough to hit anything as narrow as a man's frame?

Additionally, Marge believed the motivation for trying to kill Leroy was the same motivation for killing Dan—and Alfred was in jail at the time Leroy was run off the road.

None of the others could be eliminated as suspects in Dan's death, although the timing would have been next to impossible for Carl to leave his house, drive half an hour to Alfred's property, drug Alfred, kill Dan, and get back home to inform Angela and her Dan was dead and Alfred was being arrested. Marge also wasn't sure Jerry would have had enough time to drive from Bellevue to his father's house, get Alfred blotto, take his shotgun, and be waiting for Dan in order to shoot him. Plus, how would Jerry have known Dan was going to visit Alfred?

Hmm. *Could* it be Brent or Leroy? The only connection between them was Marge's suspicion, based on her drawings, that Brent's father might also be Dan's and Leroy's. But, she could think of no solid motive for either Brent or Leroy to kill Dan. And how would either of them have known Dan was going to visit Alfred at that particular time and with enough notice to drug Alfred and be ready to kill Dan? Besides, someone had evidently tried to kill Leroy, which made Leroy an unlikely suspect in Dan's death.

Alfred could be eliminated for the attack on Leroy,

since he was in jail. And she had been talking to Carl on the phone only minutes before she heard the sirens. It was a two-man police—or security—force, so Carl must have been in one of the two police cars roaring out of town. She breathed a sigh of relief at confirmation of the hope she could eliminate Carl as a suspect.

Leroy certainly didn't ram his own car with Jerry's, pushing his car into the ditch with him in it.

So, with this line of reasoning, it could be Brent or Jerry. Even if the timing made it impossible for Jerry to have killed Dan, he could still have run Leroy off the road.

Now Jerry was in jail. If he didn't do it, Brent was the only one left. Marge sat up straight, reaching for the phone to demand police protection for Leroy.

She pulled her hand back, shaking her head. If Brent was the murderer, he wouldn't dare try to kill Leroy now. By process of elimination, Brent should realize he could be the only suspect.

In Marge's mind, Brent was the most likely suspect, but she still couldn't figure out why. Eugene had not acknowledged paternity of Dan or Leroy; even if he was their biological father, they didn't know it, so they were not a threat to Brent. To her knowledge, no one except the mothers knew if Eugene was their father. While Marge's drawings made her pretty sure of the connection, they would be no proof to anyone else.

As she continued to sort through the facts, it came down to those two old men: one who everyone in town seemed to believe fathered Dan and Leroy and another one who Marge thought was the more likely candidate. Both Eugene and Alfred had estates to pass on, although one appeared to be of far greater value than the other. What was the value of Alfred's farm? She jotted a note to herself to check it out. If Alfred and Jerry were convicted of the crimes for which they were accused, Alfred's estate could end up with Carl and possibly Eric.

The value of Eugene's estate was so large she didn't think the exact amount made any difference. Plus, she didn't think there was any doubt who would inherit it.

This afternoon she would concentrate on finding out what she could about Alfred's estate to determine if it was worth an amount great enough to be a motivation for murder. And, if she hadn't heard from Eugene's attorney by tomorrow morning, she would call Mr. Leonard to see if there was anything he learned when he visited the Martell home.

Feeling as if she was on a roll, Marge grabbed her cell phone and headed out to her Honda. Before reaching the car, she hit the speed dial number she had put in for Cynthia. What would she have done without her trusty librarian's help?

"I'm going to the library in Pasco now. What can you tell me about looking up public records?"

"Only that it can take a day or more to do it. What are you looking for?"

Marge stopped in her tracks, deflated. She didn't have a day or two. "Anything to do with Alfred Landon's farm, his vineyard, his life insurance, his wife's life insurance, anything to do with his estate."

"Anything someone might kill for?" Cynthia asked.

"Exactly."

"Why don't you ask Alfred?"

"I can't wait around for the next visiting day at the county jail. I didn't realize how hard it would be to communicate with someone who is locked up. And now it sounds as if I can't get information from the library today, either."

The line was silent for a moment. "Why don't you come back here? I'll see if Carl has a way to get some information for us. Do you know if Alfred has an attorney?"

"If you can convince Carl to try. He is a bit unhappy with me right now. I don't know if Alfred has an attorney—it seems likely he'd have one. It would be great if he does and we could find out who it is. He would probably have most of the information I need, or he would know where to get it." Marge's spirits started to rise. "Shall we start calling around again?"

Cynthia laughed. "We could call around. We probably wouldn't have to roam as far as we did for Eugene Martell. But let's see if we can get Carl to tell us first."

"Okay. I'm still in Pasco; so I'll see you in about half an hour."

Marge headed out on Route 395, exiting at Route 17. A few minutes later, she turned onto the gravel road that would take her past the Martell and Whiting homes on her way into Dusty.

A billowing plume of dust announced a car moving way too fast on the dry gravel and dirt road. The plume grew larger, making Marge realize it was headed in her direction. She frowned and checked to be sure all her windows were tightly closed. Squinting through the dust as the car approached, she recognized the BMW logo. Who would drive such an expensive car so fast it could be damaged by flying gravel? As they drew parallel, she tried to get a look at the driver. He was staring back at her but she had to jerk her eyes to the road and grasp the steering wheel to keep from going off into the ditch, so she didn't have time to register what he looked like. She wanted to get to Dusty quickly and sketch whatever she had seen. Her fingers would remember more than her eyes did.

Marge heard the squeal of brakes behind her and the strewing of stones. She glanced in the rearview mirror. The BMW was making a fast, tight U-turn. Her heart raced and she pressed the accelerator. What was he doing? Why was he coming back this way? She hadn't done anything wrong.

Before she had time to process what was happening, the BMW pulled up beside her for a second before pulling ahead and veering into the lane directly in front of her. Marge wrenched the steering wheel to the right and stomped on the brake. She took a deep breath to ease the constriction in her chest after the Honda came to a jarring stop, only slightly tilted into a shallow ditch at the side of the road.

Looking over at the BMW, the relief fled. A man threw open the car door and charged toward her. Her eyes widened. It was Brent Martell. Was he about to kill her, too? She locked the doors and looked around for something she could use to protect herself. Nothing. But why would he want to kill her? He stopped beside the car and glared until she lowered the window a crack so she could hear him but he couldn't get in.

"You're the broad who is hounding the Whitings and invaded my home!"

It wasn't a question, so she didn't answer. She stared at him and held onto the steering wheel as if it were a lifeline.

"I'm warning you—my property is off limits. If you come around again, I've instructed Hugo he's allowed to shoot. And if he misses, I'll have you prosecuted for trespassing."

Brent spun on his heel and marched back to the BMW, started it with a roar, made another U-turn, and headed back in the direction he had been going.

# TWENTY

~~~~~~~

Marge sat for a good five minutes with her head against her hands on the steering wheel, waiting for her breathing to return to normal. When she felt steady enough to drive, she inched the Honda back onto the road and drove slowly toward Dusty, ears tuned for any unusual noises indicating she had sustained damage from the jarring stop. Hearing none, she patted the steering wheel. "Good girl," she whispered. "Thank you, Lord," she added.

Parking in front of the library, Marge walked on shaky legs to the police station. "Is Carl here?" she asked the man behind the desk.

"Nope. He's out patrolling. Can I help you?"

"I want to report ..." What did she want to report? Could one be arrested for reckless driving and intimidation? More to the point, would anyone in this town arrest Brent Martell for anything? Besides, even in the unlikely event Carl was inclined to take action, why would she report it to someone who had no real authority? "Uh, never mind. I'll talk to Carl the next time I see him." If he would ever see her again.

Her legs were steadier by the time she made her way to the library.

"Oh, good, you're here," Cynthia said as soon as Marge walked in. "I talked with Carl. He wouldn't, I quote, 'waste his time' trying to get information from Alfred Landon, but he did give me Alfred's attorney's name. I called him, and he has time to see you in about fifteen minutes."

"In Dusty?" Marge asked, startled. She didn't think there was anything like a law firm in the small town.

Cynthia laughed. "Yes, in dreary, little Dusty. He is part of a firm in Kennewick, but he lives in Dusty and does local business from a home office."

"I didn't call Dusty dreary," Marge objected. "Actually, I think it normally is a nice community."

Cynthia nodded. "Yes, even if he did it to feed his ego, the mayor started something good here. I hope we can keep it going."

Marge mulled over Cynthia's words as she followed the librarian's directions onto a dirt road that took a couple of sharp turns before delivering her to a small, fairly new, housing development not visible from the main street through town. It appeared the population of Dusty was a little larger than she had thought.

Some planning had gone into the neighborhood's design. Far from being the type of cookie-cutter development common a few years ago, each house was different. Marge saw a small cape code on the corner, two ranch houses in different colors and styles, a couple of split-levels, and even a block of row houses. Or maybe this neighborhood was fancy enough to call them townhouses.

Marge located the house she was looking for, one of the split-levels, where the attorney met her at the door and ushered her down the half-flight of stairs to an area probably meant to be a family room. On one side of the room two loveseats faced each other across a coffee table, making it feel like a living room. The other side of the room was like a dining room, with a large conference table and plush chairs. Several large paintings of eastern Washington crops in bloom adorned the walls.

Was this an office? Where were the desk, file cabinets, and bookshelves? Glancing through the open door of what would normally be a bedroom she saw them. The attorney had turned the bedroom into a working office, allowing for this pleasant space in which to interview clients.

"Good afternoon, Mrs. Peterson. My name is George Miller. Please make yourself comfortable."

Marge took a seat across from George Miller on one of the loveseats. The coffee table was laden with a carafe of what smelled like a heavenly brew of coffee accompanied by a platter of assorted pastries.

"The Dusty Café?" Marge asked, pointing to the platter.

The attorney grinned. "Guilty as charged. I live here alone. My wife passed away a few years ago, so I make good use of the wonderful cooks and bakers at the café. I take credit for the coffee, though. Please, help yourself."

Marge took an immediate liking to George Miller, studying him while he poured her a cup of coffee. He had a full head of soft, white hair. With the twinkle in his light-blue eyes, it was hard to tell his age, especially because the only wrinkles on his face seemed to be from smiling and laughing.

As soon as they were settled with coffee and pastries, he began. "I decided it would be best if I talked with Alfred before you arrived. As you know, there is very little I could tell you without his permission. Fortunately, since he has been incarcerated for a while, the real Alfred Landon responded rather than the town drunk. He has given me permission to tell you whatever you need to know, and will have his permission sent to me in writing as soon as possible, given the delays inherent in the jail system. He thinks his life is finished, and probably Jerry's as well; all he wants now is whatever is best for his grandson, Eric. We will proceed on faith that I will get the written permission."

"I can't tell you how grateful I am—to Alfred and you. The point of my investigation is to find out the truth. I don't know if Alfred is guilty—actually, I think it has been a little too convenient to assume he is. His grandson needs to know the truth, whichever way it goes."

"So, how can I help you?"

"First, a rumor has evidently been going around for years about Alfred's late wife and her life insurance. Is it true she had a large insurance policy from which he benefited?"

"Not true. Marilyn had only a small life insurance policy, taken out by Alfred, with Jerry as beneficiary and Alfred as trustee."

Marge blinked. "What happened to the money?"

"It is still in the account Alfred set up, earning interest for Jerry. Alfred never touched it and he never turned it over to Jerry. I guess he knew where it would go if he had. Unfortunately, he knew next to nothing about investing and trusted no one or it would be a sizable sum by now."

"How small is small?"

"It was for $50,000. It is now worth about $65,000."

"A fair amount, but only a desperate person would kill for it."

The attorney nodded his agreement and waited for Marge to continue.

"Second, another rumor claims Alfred's farm is worth a great deal of money, possibly because of oil or gas or some other valuable resource."

Mr. Miller laughed. "No, no such luck. Stories of oil and gas or other resources crop up in this area frequently. Despite numerous attempts to find them, none has been successful."

Marge frowned. "As much as Alfred drinks, he couldn't have been working."

Mr. Miller raised his brows, waiting.

"So, how did he pay for his liquor?"

The attorney cocked his head to the side, grinning. "Not 'how did he live?'"

"Sorry. Of course that's what I meant, but the liquor had to be a big drain on his income."

"You were out at the farm, right?"

"Yes."

"You must have noticed the grape vines, well-tended and surrounding the homestead on three sides."

"Yes, I did." Marge wondered why it hadn't struck her before. Alfred wouldn't be the one who took care of the vineyard. Whoever did probably paid Alfred for the use of the land.

"I brokered a deal with one of the local wineries to use Alfred's land. Which, unfortunately, means he can always afford the booze. Still, at least he hasn't starved to death. And, whoever inherits his land will have a money maker until they decide what to do with it. It won't make them rich, but it can provide a steady source of income."

"So, the next question is, who *does* inherit from Alfred?"

"Jerry. In one of his more lucid moments, Alfred indicated he wanted to change his will to leave everything to Eric, but he never got around to doing it; so, as of today, if something happened to Alfred, Jerry would inherit everything."

Marge frowned. "Nothing for Carl?"

"No, he felt Carl would be well taken care of by the Whitings."

"If Jerry is convicted of trying to kill Leroy, or of manslaughter or murder if Leroy dies, does he still inherit?"

The attorney nodded. "He did not gain the inheritance as a result of his actions, so I would say yes."

"Unless Alfred was Leroy's father, then Leroy would have a claim to the estate."

Mr. Miller was shaking his head. "No. Leroy has no claim to the estate. If Alfred died without a will, and paternity to Leroy could be proven, perhaps. But, he does have a will and it leaves everything to Jerry."

Marge sat back. She was out of questions. "Thank you, Mr. Miller. I'm not sure if I'm any closer to finding the truth of what happened, but your answers have ruled out a few things. May I ask a question of a different nature, purely out of curiosity?"

"Of course," George Miller said, his smile warm and grandfatherly. "What would you like to know?"

"How did this lovely neighborhood happen in the midst of what I understand at one time was almost a ghost town?"

He laughed. "I'm sure by now you've heard of our 'mayor.' He evidently had dreams of building some kind of utopia. I believe this neighborhood was to be one of several, each with its own recreational center. Ours has a pool, tennis courts, and a children's playground, among other amenities."

"I noticed he also made use of both wind power and solar power at his home. Did he build those into this community, too?"

"He did. Our windmills are deliberately hidden from view, but every home has solar panels on its roof. He was an engineer by training, gained valuable computer experience at Microsoft, and was using everything he knew to build a community for the future."

"Was?"

"Eugene had a stroke about a year ago. He has been out of sight since then, but until recently he kept tabs on all of his projects from home. Now it appears he is turning the reins over to Brent, who has stopped progress on everything Eugene wasn't obligated to by contract. Which makes all of us worry about what will become of our community after Eugene is gone."

"Will you be representing Alfred at his trial?"

The attorney shook his head. "No. I've found a competent criminal defense attorney for him. Since Alfred has so far been unable to tell us anything to defend himself, we may have to settle for diminished capacity." He handed Marge his business card. "But if you think of any more questions or you find something to help his case, please contact me."

Driving out of the carefully maintained community, Marge thought what a shame it would be to have it die from neglect. Unfortunately, one man's dreams often died with him, unless another person was willing to take over and continue.

Right now her worry was not about the town's survival.

Her main concern was to find out if Eric's father and grandfather were criminals. With this line of questioning getting her nowhere, how was she going to do it?

It had all started with Dan's murder. Why did Dan go to Alfred Landon's? To apologize was possible, but it didn't really make a lot of sense. Maybe he thought Alfred knew who his father was, and would tell Dan, even though his own mother wouldn't.

But still, Alfred had no reason to kill Dan. Who did? And how did they know Dan would be at Alfred's?

Her mind was going in circles. With no better idea, she drove to the Landon farm, parked near the barn, and stepped out of the Honda. Jerry's Impala was gone and it was quiet.

How many acres did Alfred own? Pulling George Miller's card from her pocket, she dialed his number on her cell phone.

"George Miller here."

"I have two questions for you," she said. "How many acres does Alfred own? I see nothing but grapevines surrounding the property. And is the land valuable enough for someone to be trying to get rid of heirs?"

"Alfred owns fifty acres," Mr. Miller said. "The land is fairly valuable, but if someone wanted to get it, wouldn't they kill Alfred and Jerry rather than Dan and Leroy?"

"Not if they believed Dan and Leroy were Alfred's biological offspring. Killing Dan and Leroy and putting the blame on Alfred and Jerry might be a clever thing to do to prevent any possible future claim on the property. Even if such misdirection worked, however, whoever it is would still have to deal with Eric and Carl." A chill shot through

Marge at the idea of Eric's life in jeopardy. Once again, she was grateful he was back in Bellevue under Pete's watchful eye. "Thank you. I'll probably have more questions later."

As soon as Marge disconnected with the attorney she punched in Carl's number. To her surprise, he answered.

"Yes, Marge. What do you need now?"

"I don't need anything at the moment, thank you," she said in as sweet a voice as she could manage. "But you need to be extra careful until this situation is resolved."

She explained her reasoning for the warning.

After a moment of silence, Carl barked a derisive laugh. She could almost see his head shaking. "Why can't you accept the fact that two drunks did irrational things?"

"What about Brent Martell running me off the road a couple hours ago and warning me to stay away?" she argued.

"He *what*? Why is this the first I'm hearing about it? I can't blame him much though, with you sticking your nose in where it doesn't belong … but I'll have a talk with him about it."

Marge wished she'd kept her mouth shut. What good would talking do? She hit the disconnect button hard. Slamming down the receiver of an old-fashioned landline phone would have been much more satisfying. She had been right. Carl wasn't about to rock the boat with Brent Martell. Was she really glad she had eliminated Carl as a suspect? Especially since it now appeared he might inherit a fairly valuable property. Did the Whitings still live in Dusty because they couldn't afford to move? Was Carl looking for his future with the Landon vineyards?

If Jerry didn't inherit because he was in prison, would Alfred's estate be split between Eric and Carl? Maybe

Jerry would write his own will and leave everything to Eric. Marge didn't think Carl would even contemplate getting rid of Eric in order to inherit the whole thing himself. She shook her head. Who knew what anyone would do for money?

Shoving her cell phone in a pocket, Marge started walking around Alfred's property with no idea what she might find. She looked through the dilapidated barn, its doors hanging off the hinges. Eric would be disappointed. The 1970 Chevy pickup he had admired in the newspaper article wasn't in the barn. She looked into the tool shed where Eric had hidden while the house was being searched.

Climbing the steps to the front door of the house, Marge almost knocked. Laughing at herself, she tried the doorknob and was surprised to find the door unlocked. Had the police not been back to check the house since Jerry was taken into custody? Probably not. The house was not part of the crime scene for the attack on Leroy, and they had already been through it to look for Eric.

Not sure what she was doing or why, Marge stepped into the house quietly, as if someone might hear her. She went into the basement where she had hidden with Eric. It was as she remembered, except it felt darker and danker. After a quick look around, she decided Eric had taken everything worth keeping. All she found was a stash of whiskey. Either Alfred forgot about it, or it was there in case a snowstorm or something kept him from getting new supplies. She felt a sneeze coming and decided to get out of the damp basement.

The air on the first floor wasn't much better. Three giant

sneezes shook her before she could continue. How long had it been since anyone had done any housecleaning? Holding one hand to her nose, Marge started through the house. She wished she dared open a few windows to get rid of the horrible odor.

A rustling in the corner nearly sent Marge screaming for the door. She took a shallow breath, gritted her teeth, and pushed herself forward. She had no idea what she was searching for, but she stood in the middle of the kitchen and looked around. Logically, she had no reason to worry about the state of the house, but as long as she was here she might as well do something about it. Finding some large trash bags buried in the back of the pantry, she emptied the refrigerator. From the condition of the food inside, it must have been turned off for a while. Any food in the pantry that would attract more varmints than were already there followed the refrigerator contents into the bag. She propped the door of the refrigerator open, emptied a box of baking soda of indeterminate age into a bowl, and put it on a shelf. She wouldn't let herself go all housewifely and clean the darn thing, tempting as it was.

It felt good to be doing something even though it was probably useless, so Marge took another bag and tackled the living and dining room area. It was almost as bad as the refrigerator. Numerous empty whiskey bottles; ashtrays overflowing with cigarette butts; paper plates and TV meal trays, many with uneaten food still in them, were strewn about the floor and furniture. She found nothing of interest, so the bag of trash joined the two from the kitchen outside the kitchen door.

Grabbing yet another garbage bag, she went into what

she thought would be an office or den, but was what Alfred had evidently used as his bedroom. There wasn't much to find here, except for more overflowing ashtrays and mounds of dirty clothes. It was a wonder Alfred hadn't burned the place down. Avoiding the clothes, she emptied the ashtrays and went up the stairs, wondering whether Alfred had restricted his activity to the lower level.

A loud creak on the third step made her stop, heart pounding. How many creaking stairs did this place have? Anyone in the house would know exactly where she was. She shook her head. No one was here. She would have heard or seen something by now if there were.

When Marge opened the door of the first room on the second floor, she caught her breath. She couldn't take a garbage bag reeking of stale tobacco into that sanctuary—it would be like committing sacrilege. A fine coating of dust covered everything, from the photos of Marilyn Landon that covered the walls to the books on spirituality, candles, and incense burners on the tables. It was the amount of dust one would expect after being away on vacation, not after years of accumulation. Alfred had obviously continued taking care of his wife the only way he could after she was gone.

Marge backed out and closed the door carefully behind her. Alfred's shrine to his wife wiped out any lingering suspicion that he might have killed her.

The next bedroom had to be Jerry's. A few mementos from his childhood were strewn in disarray, along with more piles of dirty clothes. She found nothing of interest in his closets or drawers. Jerry had at least piled his bottles and emptied his ashtrays into the wastebasket. Marge dumped them into her trash bag and continued down the hall.

The third bedroom was the master, and it didn't appear to have been used or even entered in years, possibly since Marilyn's death. Cobwebs clung to every surface and the coating of dust was thick and sneeze-inducing. Marge backed out and closed the door as quickly as she could.

Standing in the doorway of the last room, Marge's eyes narrowed. The only furniture was a desk and chair in the middle of the room. Three file boxes sat in a row beside the desk. On top of the desk were two neatly stacked piles of paper. No computer. Marge guessed Alfred never entered the computer age.

Had Alfred been using this room for his office after turning the den downstairs into his bedroom? Perhaps he came up here in his lucid moments, when he was sober and trying to gain custody of his grandson. That would explain the neatness of the desktop.

Marge walked in. If she found answers to any of her questions in the house, they would be in this room. However, if she were Jerry, she would have been curious about Alfred's affairs and gone through his papers.

Marge walked to the desk. Alfred was either a highly functional alcoholic or he managed a lot when he was on the wagon. The first stack of papers contained bank statements and utility and other bills for the running of the house. The second stack contained the contract and payment records from the winery leasing his fields. It wasn't a huge amount, but more than enough to take care of Alfred's needs. She shook her head. Had she expected to find anything here, in plain sight, which would answer her questions?

Marge used the edge of the garbage bag to cover her hand and open the first file box. The papers in it were yellowed and fragile. The tabs on the folders indicated the files ranged from Alfred's parents' marriage to Alfred's own wedding, and included Alfred's school and medical records. She would guess Alfred's parents had filed these records. She put the lid back on and went to the next box. The folders in this one contained old financial records. They might be too old to have any bearing on the case. Anyway, it would take time to go through them, and she didn't dare take them with her to do it. The third box was barely a quarter full. It contained more records about Alfred's marriage, his parents' deaths, and Jerry's birth. Alfred had evidently stopped keeping any personal records after the death of his wife. Marge leafed through it quickly, but it appeared nothing had been added after Marilyn's death.

Marge wished she could take possession of these boxes long enough to put together some kind of family history for Eric. She went back to the first box and gently leafed through the folders. Noticing one that had appeared to slip down beneath the others, she pulled it out. She stared at it, confused. This folder was not old and fragile – it was new and had no identification on the tab.

Opening the folder, she gasped. She was looking at Alfred's will, and he had been in the process of making changes to it. Alfred had crossed off Jerry's name as beneficiary of his estate and replaced it with Eric's name. Of special interest was a handwritten paragraph admitting paternity to Carl Whiting and stating that he felt Carl was well taken care of by his grandparents and neither needed nor wanted anything from Alfred.

In another paragraph, he declared Jerry and Carl were his only sons and that he was not the father of Dan or Leroy. He also wrote that their natural father had taken care of them in the past and would undoubtedly do right by them in his own will.

What did Alfred mean by that? What did he know? And why wasn't he telling?

She pulled out her cell phone and called George Miller to inform him of what she had found. She didn't think it was legally binding, since it hadn't been completed and witnessed, but it did show Alfred's intent. He had no reason to kill Dan, and Jerry had no reason to attack Leroy.

There was no signal. She remembered the first day, during her confrontation with Alfred when she tried to call 911 and didn't have a signal. She would have to go back out by the barn, where she had been able to call Mr. Miller and Carl earlier. As she turned to go, a familiar creak from the direction of the stairs stopped her.

# TWENTY-ONE

Marge's head jerked toward the door. Who would be in the house? The police? No. If they were going to search the house they would have done so by now. She shoved the folder with the papers Alfred had been working on into the garbage bag and looked around in panic. The closet? She tiptoed over and opened the door. No hiding there—it was empty. Hearing footsteps stop in the doorway behind her, she whirled around, trying to look more startled than terrified. Terrified won when she found herself staring into the barrel of a gun.

After what seemed like the longest moment Marge had ever endured, the gun lowered.

"What are you doing here?" Carl asked.

"What are you doing here?" she countered.

"I'm on police business. *You* are trespassing."

Marge's eyes narrowed. "Police business? Did you get a search warrant?"

Carl sighed. "I have permission from Alfred, remember? Your turn."

Marge bit her tongue to keep from questioning Carl's sudden interest in this house, which was not really part of a crime he insisted was already solved, his authority to investigate a crime at all, and whether he could stretch that permission from Alfred to be here when Eric had already been found. "Well, you are kind of late getting around to the house. I thought it would be worth a look, but mostly I have been collecting trash. I already have three bags full. I decided to check in this closet to see if there was something more I should get rid of to keep the varmints from invading, but there is nothing in it." Marge realized she was chattering and clamped her mouth shut.

Carl leaned back on his heels, a grin on his face. "So, now you're a housekeeper?"

"Well, I was looking for evidence, too. I was going to see what was in those file boxes and on the desk." Marge almost bit her tongue. Did she have to mention the file boxes? And when had lies started slipping out of her mouth so easily?

"I'll handle those," Carl stated. "You can take your trash and leave. I'm giving you a warning now, but the next time I find you trespassing you'll be arrested."

Marge scurried out of the house before Carl could change his mind. She panicked when she remembered she had left the lid off the box in which she had found the folder. As soon as Carl noticed he would suspect she had removed something. She had every intention of giving the papers to him. But she knew she'd never see them again after she did, so she needed to make a copy of them first.

Jumping into the Honda, she sped into Dusty and parked in front of the library. She pulled the folder out of the trash bag and waved it around to get rid of any ashes while she ran through the library door, raising a hand in Cynthia's direction on her way to the copier.

Once she had copied the pages of the will Alfred had

been working on, she folded the copies and stuck them in her purse before walking over to talk with Cynthia while keeping an eye on the library door. Two minutes later Carl came charging in.

"Where is it?"

"Where is what?"

He eyed the folder in Marge's hands.

"Did you take that folder from the Landon house?"

"Oh, this. Yes, I did. Why? Do you want it?"

"You know I do," he barked, holding out his hand.

Marge silently handed him the folder. He grabbed it and strode out of the library. Marge turned to Cynthia, whose eyes were wide.

"What was he in such a snit about?" Cynthia asked.

Marge shrugged. "I found a copy of Alfred's will. He had been in the process of making some changes to it and I wanted to make a copy of the changes for Mr. Miller before giving it to Carl."

"In Alfred's house? Were you breaking and entering?"

"No breaking. The door wasn't locked. I did enter, though."

"How was Alfred changing his will?"

Marge bit her lip. "I'd like to tell you, but it is probably confidential information I shouldn't have and certainly shouldn't share. I'm going to get it over to Alfred's attorney now."

Exiting the library quickly to avoid Cynthia's hurt look, Marge pulled out her cell phone. She hated keeping anything from Cynthia, since the librarian had been so helpful, but she was quite sure it wasn't appropriate to tell Cynthia what was in the will. A call to George Miller verified he would be in his office the rest of the afternoon. Marge's heart was still racing when she pulled away from the curb. She had to force herself to slow down for the drive to the attorney's house.

~

"Unfortunately, this doesn't change anything," Mr. Miller confirmed when he had looked over the papers Marge handed him. "Legally, in the state of Washington, changes can't be made to a will by crossing out and filling in. They must be done in an addendum and signed by two witnesses. It also isn't proof, but it does seem to verify Dan and Leroy were not Alfred's sons. I'll keep this in his file in case we ever need to substantiate his intentions."

"It would help if we could figure out if whoever killed Dan knew Dan wasn't Alfred's son," Marge said. "Something about the way he wrote the last paragraph makes me believe Alfred knows who Dan and Leroy's biological father is and that they shared the same father."

Mr. Miller nodded. "I agree. I'll see if Alfred's defense attorney can get any information from him."

Marge returned to her car in deep thought. She had her doubts about Alfred being willing to talk. Granted, he was in a difficult situation right now, but the case against him wasn't based on whether or not he was Dan's father. The charge was manslaughter, based on his being drunk and shooting someone he claimed he thought was a trespasser. Since he had no recollection of the event, he couldn't deny it. It would do him no good to disclose what, if anything, he knew about Dan's father.

So what could she do now? Marge pulled up in front of the Dusty Café. Maybe an early dinner would help her think about her next steps.

The waitress greeted Marge with a smile. Marge felt like she was becoming a regular customer, which was much more comfortable than being an anonymous customer in a different restaurant. Her cell phone rang while she was still looking over the menu.

"Mrs. Peterson?"

"Yes."

"This is Ron Leonard." His voice sounded perturbed. "I thought I should let you know that I attempted to see Eugene Martell today. His son informed me he was too ill to talk with anyone, including his attorney. This is not acceptable, so tomorrow I will speak with his physician to see what I can find out. I need to verify whether Brent has taken over decision-making for his father based on Eugene's inability to handle his own affairs or if he is acting on instructions from Eugene. If Eugene is unable to handle his affairs, I will have to inform Brent that he does not have power of attorney for his father. I do. Once he knows the facts, Brent can either let me in voluntarily or I can get legal help to do so."

"Oh," Marge gasped. "I wonder why Mr. Martell wouldn't give his son power of attorney."

"I'm not at liberty to talk about Eugene's personal business. But he made the change from his son to me about three months ago."

"Thank you, Mr. Leonard. I was planning on getting in touch with you in the morning if I hadn't heard from you. I would like to show you some sketches I made. They might shed some light on the whole situation. When may I see you?"

"I'll want to speak with Eugene's physician to determine what the situation is and whether we need to take any action before I consider discussing anything more with you."

"Of course, I understand," Marge said. Her sketches proved nothing, anyway. Only her suspicions wouldn't go away.

Soon after Marge ordered the night's special of Thai Ginger Beef, the biggest surprise to her on the menu, Cynthia walked in the door and over to her table.

"Thought I might find you here," she said.

"Please, sit down. Do you have time to stay for a bite with me?"

"No, but I'll have a cup of coffee so we can chat a minute." Cynthia signaled to the waitress and settled in the chair across from Marge.

"Quite an eclectic menu," Marge said. "I didn't expect to find Thai food on this side of the mountains."

"We have a highly trained chef," Cynthia said. "You have probably noticed by now Eugene Martell never did anything halfway."

"He must pay a good salary to attract such talent to a small town," Marge said. "I wonder if the café can make it on its own if Eugene dies."

Cynthia shook her head, frowning. "A great deal of this town could be in danger when he no longer holds the reins," she said. "I have no idea if Eugene's housing and commercial developments have progressed enough to support the town without him."

The door opened again, and Carl charged in, spotted Marge, strode over to her table, pulled out a chair, and sat.

"Still on duty?" Marge asked.

"And likely to be for some time," he said. He appeared to control his voice with difficulty. "What did you tell Eugene's attorney that has Brent so upset?"

"Nothing! At least nothing I hadn't already told you. I guess his attorney decided to do something about it. Don't tell me Brent has complained because Ron Leonard asked to see his own client."

"And you know he went there because …?"

"Because Mr. Leonard called and told me. He also told me Brent stonewalled him. I wonder why."

"So now it's called 'stonewalling' when trying to protect your sick father?"

"Has Eugene's doctor confirmed he is too sick to see his attorney?"

Carl sighed. "Everyone in Dusty knows Eugene has a terminal illness and isn't expected to live more than a few months."

Marge swallowed. Was it possible Brent was only protecting his father and not deliberately isolating him for his own reasons? She shook her head. The man she had seen in the upstairs window of the Martell mansion was asking for help. She was sure of it. But how could she prove it?

"Has Eugene's doctor ever indicated Eugene needed someone to take power of attorney for him?"

"How would I have information about Eugene's affairs? I presume Brent is handling them."

"Well, Mr. Leonard is taking steps to see Mr. Martell tomorrow. After they have talked and Mr. Leonard is satisfied his needs are being met, Brent will have no cause for concern."

"Brent is Eugene's son. If Brent is satisfied Eugene's needs are being met, why should anyone else interfere?" Carl's voice had gone up a notch. He was clearly having difficulty controlling his temper.

"Because Brent isn't the deciding voice. Ron Leonard has power of attorney for Eugene if he is incapacitated." Marge cringed. Had she just accidentally divulged privileged information?

Both Carl and Cynthia stared at her.

"I'm sorry. I shouldn't have told you. Mr. Leonard informed me Eugene changed his instructions a few months ago to switch the power of attorney from Brent to himself. So Brent has to allow Mr. Leonard to see Mr. Martell and make the determination whether to take whatever steps are necessary to activate it."

Carl scraped his chair back, stood, and strode out of the café after a final glare at Marge.

"Whew!" Cynthia breathed. "I don't think I've ever seen Carl that angry."

Marge's own anger was bubbling just beneath the surface; she took a few deep breaths to calm it. "What does he have to be angry about? The possibility he might not be right about everything?"

"He is dealing with a lot, Marge. Maybe he hasn't been close to Alfred and Jerry all these years, but they are his father and brother, and he's had to put them in jail."

"He seemed happy to do it," shot out of Marge's mouth before she thought about what she was saying.

She clamped her jaw shut. What a terribly judgmental

thing to say. Cynthia was right. She couldn't know what Carl was feeling. And he had been so good to Eric and her before she started interfering with the investigation.

Cynthia stood to leave.

"I'm sorry," Marge said. "That wasn't called for, and you are right."

"No problem. We all have our days."

Marge was relieved to see Cynthia's smile and small wave as she left the restaurant. She hoped it indicated Cynthia meant what she said.

Marge's Thai Ginger Beef arrived. Still perturbed, she said a quick grace and dove in. After two bites, she put her fork down and took a few more deep breaths. It was too good to shovel in without tasting. Besides, she needed to get her equilibrium back if she was going to figure out what to do next. Picking up her fork, she returned to her food at a more sedate pace and did, indeed, enjoy every bite.

Marge walked out of the restaurant into the lingering daylight of summer without a plan for what to do next. Her drive back to Pasco took her past the Martell mansion—somehow she found herself parked behind a rise and walking to where she had a view of the house without being seen. What did she expect to find?

What she saw startled her. Was the vehicle parked near the front door an ambulance? It was shaped like one although it had no markings or emergency lights, only a logo on the side she couldn't read from where she stood.

While she watched, two men rolled a gurney out of the front door and slid it into the back of the vehicle. A man with white hair was strapped to the gurney. The men climbed in the cab and, with a quick tap on the horn, started driving away. Brent quickly emerged from the house, got into his BMW, and followed it down the driveway. Marge waited impatiently for Hugo to return inside the house and close the door behind him before she raced back to her car to follow.

Marge was thankful that both the approaching darkness and the sedate pace at which they were traveling prevented her from creating a visible dust cloud, possibly giving away her presence. She stayed well back on the lightly used road to avoid detection.

Pulling out her cell phone, she called Carl. Fortunately, she had him on speed dial because she wasn't accustomed to using the phone while driving. The call went to voicemail.

"Brent is having Eugene moved from the house in a gray vehicle shaped like an ambulance. It has lettering or a logo on the side but I couldn't read it," she said. "I'm following as long as I can."

She was grateful Mr. Leonard had called her earlier, so she could place a return call without having to look up his number. It also went to voicemail and she repeated her message. Disconnecting, she put both hands back on the wheel.

The two vehicles in front of her turned left onto Route 17, driving away from Pasco. Where were they going? They were traveling a couple of miles over the speed limit, the way many people do. Marge allowed other cars to pass her, creating a barrier, and she stayed far enough behind to make sure she wasn't noticed and would not be recognized if the traffic lessened and hers was the only car left behind them.

Marge wracked her brain about who else she could

contact. The number she had for Cynthia was the library's, and Cynthia wouldn't be there this late. The only other person whose number she had was Angela's. She took a breath, picked up her cell phone again, and managed to page down through recent calls to find Angela's number.

Marge started talking before Angela had time to say hello.

"Just listen, please. I don't know how long I can talk. Brent is moving his father, I don't know where. I'm following them north on Route 17. I can't reach Carl or Eugene's attorney. Please try to get to Carl as soon as possible and have him call me."

"Marge …"

The two vehicles had sped up. Had they seen her? She'd have to take a chance and also accelerate so she didn't lose them.

"I can't talk now, Angela. Get me some help. Please."

# TWENTY-TWO

～～～～～

Marge disconnected and gripped the steering wheel. Her foot came down hard on the accelerator until the gap between the vehicles narrowed. Adrenaline surged through her as she jerked her foot back off. She had over-compensated for their change of speed.

Her breath was ragged because of the tightness in her chest. If only dark came earlier in July, she might be able to stay hidden. What would Brent do if he spotted her?

The ambulance continued steadily at the slightly faster speed and Marge finally relaxed, realizing they had only adjusted their speed to what most people drove on this road.

Were they headed for I-90 or going to Moses Lake? Neither. They turned right onto an unmarked road shortly after crossing Route 26.

The side road would have little or no traffic. It would be far too easy for them to spot Marge's Honda if she made the turn directly behind them. She passed the turnoff and drove for about a quarter mile before finding a spot where she could make a U-turn. She got back to the cross-street and made a careful left, squinting ahead in the gather-ing dusk. She couldn't see either the ambulance or Brent's BMW. Had she lost them? She was tempted to speed up but thought better of it. The road appeared to be flat and straight as far as she could see. Taillights should still be visible. Most likely, while she was still on the main road, they turned off on a side street or driveway. Shoulders tense, she slowed to a crawl, peering in at every trail and driveway she passed.

Her breath came out in a small explosion when, after the first curve in the road, she spotted the BMW on her left, half hidden by trees, parked on a driveway in front of a large, rambling building. Trying to stay calm, she continued around the curve until she was sure her Honda couldn't be seen, grabbed her cell phone, quietly got out of her car, and crept toward the building through a clump of trees. Now she could see the ambulance backed into the driveway. Its rear door was open and the gurney had been removed. A sign on the building read Hidden Valley Nursing Home.

All she needed to know was where Brent had taken his father. Now it was time to get out of there, before Brent saw her. She would direct the authorities to the nursing home and let them handle it. Turning toward her car, she had only taken a few steps when her cell phone rang. She froze. Why hadn't she thought to put it on vibrate?

A glance over her shoulder proved Brent had heard and was headed in her direction. Heart in her throat, she started to run while punching the answer button on her phone. "Help me," she whispered. "Brent has seen me. I won't be able to get to my car before he catches me. Turn right after route 26. Hidden Valley Nursing Home is about three miles in on the left."

Leaving the connection open, she slipped the phone in

her pocket and pretended to trip, throwing her arms out as if to keep her balance.

"My cell phone!" she cried as a hand grabbed her right arm and pinned her in place.

"You don't need it now. Why are you following me?" Brent demanded.

"Why are you hiding your father?" she retorted.

"I don't think what my father and I do is any of your business."

"Oh?" Marge tried to deflate, as if defeated. "I guess you're right. Release my arm and I'll go away."

Brent laughed, but the sound was harsh. "How is it I don't believe you? Let me walk you to your car and watch you drive away."

What was he up to? Marge didn't believe for a minute he was going to let her drive away. After a moment's thought she realized he was putting distance between them and the nursing home. A chill crept over her. She opened her mouth to scream, hoping her phone line was still open. His free hand slapped over her mouth and he pushed her forward.

When they reached the Honda, he demanded, "Give me your keys!" She tried to reply. Brent's grip on her arm tightened. "You scream and I'll break your arm," he hissed, taking his hand off her mouth.

Marge believed he would do it. She swallowed a couple of times, trying to create enough saliva to be able to talk.

"All right, you've made your point," she said. Her voice still came out in a squeak. She swallowed again and took a breath to steady herself, digging her keys out of her pocket. "I promise I'll leave and not come back."

"Not a chance. You've stuck your nose into my business once too often." He grabbed the keys and pushed her into the driver's seat. Marge hastened to obey when a gun appeared in his hand.

"What are you going to do, kill me, too?" Marge tried to steady her shaking voice. "Who do you have left to blame it on?"

"I'll cross that bridge when I come to it."

His eyes and his gun stayed trained on Marge as he rounded the front of the Honda and got into the passenger seat. He handed her the keys. "Now drive. Slowly."

She did as she was told while her mind jumped around trying to think of a maneuver to prevent him from shooting her. She couldn't think of one.

"Now stop," he said after they rounded another curve a few minutes later. Surprised, Marge obeyed. "Put your hands through the steering wheel."

Brent had removed his belt while she was driving and used it to secure her hands. After tugging it to make sure it was tight, he pulled out his cell phone and hit a speed dial button.

"Hugo? I need you. No, a couple miles down the road from there. I'm in a blue Honda. And you need to be thinking of some way to set up a fatal car crash. Don't give me any guff, just get here! Now!" After disconnecting, Brent appeared to settle in for the wait.

"Aren't they going to be looking for you back there?"

"No, I completed all the paperwork before coming. They wanted my signature to verify he was safely in the nursing home. I was about to leave when I spotted—or rather heard—you. That was pretty careless."

"It was," she admitted. She hoped her phone was still on and someone was listening. If she could keep Brent talking, he might say something more incriminating. "I'm curious. How are you going to manufacture a fatal accident out here where I have no reason to be?"

"Who said it would happen here? There's not much traffic between Dusty and Pasco in the middle of the night."

Marge started. "How did you know I was staying in Pasco?"

He laughed. "Haven't you learned yet there are no secrets in a small town?"

"You seem to have done pretty well at keeping secrets," Marge countered.

Brent shrugged. "Yeah, well, but you see, I own the town."

Marge stared at him. "I thought your father owned the town. Is that why you need to get rid of him, so you can take over?"

Brent's voice lost its dismissive tone. "I don't need to get rid of him. He's my father and I wouldn't harm him. But he is dying, so it will only be a matter of time."

"Ah, yes. Especially if you get his other sons out of the way."

Brent glared at her. "What? No. I am my father's only son."

"I don't think so. And neither do you or you wouldn't have killed Dan and tried to kill Leroy. Were you afraid they would make their claims after your father was dead? By the way, what did you give Alfred and Jerry to knock them out so completely?"

"My father has never admitted paternity to anyone but

me, and Dan and Leroy's mothers never claimed my dad was their father."

"True. And a simple DNA test on your father might prove whether or not he is. Why don't you have one done?"

"I don't need to have anything done, and I think you had better stop talking." Brent's voice was getting more strident.

"What are you going to do to stop me?"

Brent pulled his hand back as if to hit her with the pistol.

Marge's heart thudded, but she managed what she hoped was a derisive laugh. "You'd better be careful or you'll leave marks a car crash can't explain. Too bad you can't get Jerry's car involved in this one, too."

"A fire will take care of any marks nicely," Brent muttered with a nervous look at the rearview mirror.

Marge swallowed hard, the image of a fiery crash all too vivid in her mind. She had to keep him talking.

"Shooting Dan with Alfred's gun was probably easy. Alfred had no reason to suspect whatever you gave him would knock him out. Did you put it in a bottle of bourbon? But even after you drugged Jerry, using his car on Leroy was a bit trickier, wasn't it?"

"I have no idea what you are talking about," Brent said.

"And yet you are willing to kill me to keep me from talking about it," Marge said. "I wonder why."

They heard the sound of a vehicle approaching from behind. Brent leaned back and gave Marge a wicked grin. A vehicle sped around the bend, red and blue lights suddenly slicing through the dark as the driver evidently spotted them. Brent sat bolt upright. The car pulled up in front of them and another car with flashing lights stopped behind them. Brent looked at the gun in his hand as if he couldn't imagine how it got there and looked at Marge as if he wanted to give it to her before finally dropping it on the floor and kicking it under the seat.

Marge burst into laughter. She couldn't stop laughing even after Carl and the county detective unbound her hands from the steering wheel and helped her out of the car. She laughed until her side hurt at the sight of Hugo hurtling around the curve and braking with a scrunch of gravel. He reversed and executed a tight U-turn to head back in the other direction, quickly followed by a county police car.

"Do I have to slap you to get you to stop?" Carl asked, his face showing the effort it took not to join her in laughter.

"How did you find us?" Brent asked.

"She called," the county detective said.

"Before she lost the phone?" Brent asked, looking perplexed.

Marge had almost subdued her laughter, but now it came bubbling out again. She pulled her cell phone out of her pocket. "Neatest sleight of hand I've ever done," she managed between bouts of hysteria.

"I guess you were a bit scared," Carl ventured, gripping her arms.

"Just a bit," she admitted, leaning her head against his shoulder and taking deep, shuddering breaths to regain control.

"I have done nothing wrong," Brent declared at the same time an officer backed out of the Honda with the gun in a gloved hand. Now it was the detective's turn to laugh.

He took the gun and held it up before putting it in an evidence bag. He reached out for Marge's phone and slipped it into another one.

"You might want to hit disconnect now," Marge mentioned.

Brent stared at her. A mixture of disbelief and hatred flooded his face.

The detective and Carl were also staring at her. The detective pulled the phone out of the evidence bag and held it to his ear. "Is someone there?" he asked.

Marge straightened up and watched as the detective appeared to be listening to someone. A moment later he handed the phone to her.

"Hello?" she said.

"What have you gotten yourself into now," boomed across the connection.

"Pete? You are the one who called?"

"Yes, and I had enough time after I heard you struggle with someone to get a recording device and then I phoned the Benton County Police Department. The quality of the recording is pretty bad, but I'll overnight it tomorrow."

"Oh, thank goodness. I can't remember exactly what Brent said, but I'm sure it's enough to at least make them look at him for Dan's murder."

A detective walked up to Carl and Marge. He was coming back from the nursing home. "I believe Mr. Martell is safe in there," he said. "I'm leaving an officer on guard, in case I'm wrong. Mr. Martell has been heavily sedated, and the nursing home staff has written instructions to keep him sedated. They are not familiar with the physician who ordered it, however, and have agreed to hold off on giving him anything more until his regular physician can check on him, which we'll make sure is done first thing tomorrow."

Carl convinced Marge to let a deputy drive her car back to Dusty while she rode with him, giving him time to get her whole story.

~

"You could have been in deep trouble back there, trying to do police work," Carl said.

"I was only following them, and I was trying to contact you the whole time. I needed to see where they were taking Mr. Martell. I was about to leave, but unfortunately my phone rang and Brent heard it. If I hadn't followed them, no one would know where Eugene was."

Carl frowned. "We knew the general area where you were because of your previous call. And your husband called to give us your exact location while recording your conversation with Brent. Do you think you got him to say enough to incriminate himself?"

"To tell the truth, I can't remember much of the conversation. I was too scared, but I thought if I kept him talking he might let something slip. Brent certainly intended to do me harm, though, and whatever Pete recorded will probably corroborate his plans. I can only hope he did let something slip that will help the investigation into Dan's death."

Carl nodded. "Yes, it would be nice if we got something from the recording of your conversation to solve all our problems," he said.

Marge had a feeling Carl was being a little bit sarcastic.

She gave him a sideways look. "So, are you willing to consider that Alfred and Jerry might be innocent?"

"Not so fast, Marge. None of tonight's events is necessarily connected to Dan's murder or the attack on Leroy. Unless that recording really does shed new light on things, Alfred and Jerry are still the main suspects."

Marge stared at him.

"You evidently made some accusations, and you can't remember what Brent said in response," Carl continued. "We are currently not aware of anything incriminating Brent has done or admitted to so far."

"Except, maybe, trying to kill me?" Marge asked.

The look on Carl's face made Marge wonder whether he wished Brent had succeeded.

# TWENTY-THREE

~~~~~~~~

Carl was right. Despite everything Marge had discovered, and despite what she now believed to be true, they still didn't have proof Dan and Leroy were Eugene Martell's biological sons. Even if they were, why would Brent want to kill them? She had a strong feeling Eugene was the only one besides Brent who could answer those questions.

Marge wished she hadn't been so frightened she couldn't remember whether Brent had said enough while her cell phone was turned on to substantiate her claims. She could only hope he had, and the recording Pete made would give the police what they needed for evidence.

By the time they reached the Dusty police station, where the deputy had parked her Honda, Marge felt steady enough to drive to her motel. The deputy was still there, so she found a sheet of copy paper and made a quick sketch of Hugo so the county police could identify him when they caught him.

She drove slowly toward Pasco, trying to calm her thoughts enough to figure out how things stood with the investigation. She was here to find out who killed Dan, so the crime would not be left on Alfred's door if he didn't do it. She thought the question of who ran Leroy off the road would be answered at the same time. If she was right, Jerry would also be cleared. Of course, that would mean Alfred and Jerry would be free and she would probably have to fight them for custody of Eric. Especially if they maintained sobriety. Was it really wise to pursue?

Yes, it was always wise to pursue the truth. And Eric's self-esteem would take a beating if his father and grandfather were both convicted of these crimes. Even if she lost custody, Eric had to know the truth.

So, patience, she counseled herself. One step at a time. Tomorrow Eugene Martell would probably be able to explain what was going on in his life. She hoped what he said would answer all of the questions.

Of course, it might not. If by some quirk it turned out he wasn't Dan and Leroy's biological father, or if he refused to admit paternity or take a DNA test, Marge would have no choice but to return home with the questions she had unresolved.

~

Marge called Pete on the phone in her motel room. "Are you all right? What is this phone number?" he asked. "It sounded like that maniac was going to kill you."

"I'm sure he planned to," she said. "Fortunately, the police were already headed my way because of the calls I had made while I was tailing Brent and his father. Otherwise, they might not have arrived in time to stop Brent."

"I'm sorry my call drew Brent's attention to you. I wasn't expecting you to be skulking around at night. As soon as I realized your line was still open, after I heard you holler 'my cell phone,' I put my phone on speaker and began taping the call. I also called the Benton County police to pass on the location information you gave me."

"Yes, your call did alert Brent but it wasn't your fault. I should have known enough to turn off the phone before I got so close. I fooled him by pretending to lose it. I hoped the line would stay open and I could get him to say something incriminating. I'm not sure it worked, but at least what you taped proves he abducted me and was planning to kill me. That should keep him locked up for a while.

"The police have my phone now; so I'm using the motel phone. Why did they keep it? Do they need it to prove it was the phone transmitting the conversation that you recorded?"

"Possibly. If they need to keep it longer, get a new phone tomorrow and ask them to have your stored information transferred to it before you come home. We need you to come home."

"Why? Has something happened with Benjamin?"

"He hasn't come home tonight. Since we know he found his mother, there is no reason for him to be out this late. It appears both he and his mother are missing."

"Oh, Pete," Marge cried. Guilt and loss raged through her. She hadn't been there for Benjamin, and Benjamin had chosen his mother over her. Benjamin was the one who tugged at her heartstrings; her feelings for him were what had originally convinced her to foster the two boys. Now she wasn't there at the time he needed her most.

"I'm coming home tomorrow," she said. "I think I'm close to finding out the truth for Eric, but it could happen without me here."

"Come home tomorrow, but don't rush if you can help resolve things for Eric first. You being here won't help us find Benjamin any faster, but my gut says he's really going to need you when we do."

Sleep was impossible. Marge sat at the desk, her fingers flying over pages in her sketchpad. Alfred, Jerry, Carl, and Eric on one page. Such a strong resemblance among them. Brent, Dan, Leroy, and what she could remember of Eugene on another page. Yes, she was sure of it. The resemblance was not as strong as with the other set, but it was there in the shape of the jaw, the high forehead, the thrust of the chin. The eyes were different, and the mouths, but they had to be related.

She leaned back and closed her eyes. She had to assume Eugene Martell was the biological father of all three boys. He had never admitted paternity of Dan and Leroy, nor would their mothers disclose who their biological father was, preferring to let Alfred take the blame. Why? Had Eugene threatened the women somehow?

Maybe, but there was another possible explanation, one Marge thought made more sense. Eugene was a wealthy man. Wealthy enough to rebuild a town practically on his own. Wealthy enough to make it worth their while for the women to keep their mouths shut. Had he been paying them off all these years? Were they still getting money?

Did Brent find out and then decide to kill Dan and Leroy in order to stop the payments—with what he probably considered was his money since Eugene was dying? But Dan's mother still refused to reveal the identity of Dan's biological father even after Dan was killed; so were the payments continuing? Would the payments stop after

Eugene was gone? And if they did cease, would the women agree to talk then?

Marge stood and paced the room. She was beating her head against the wall for nothing. Eugene would come out of sedation tomorrow and he would be able to tell them his side of the story. After their questions were answered, she could go home and take care of Benjamin.

# TWENTY-FOUR

Pete disconnected with Marge and shook his head. He was getting almost as good at dissembling as she was. Yes, it was getting late. No, Ben had not come home. But he hadn't told Marge Eric was also gone.

He knew where Eric was, of course, in a general way. He was out on the dark streets, the dangerous streets, looking for Ben. Eric and Pete had argued about it and, overconfident in his position as always, Pete thought he had convinced Eric that a twelve-year-old did not belong out on the streets. The police would handle it.

What he had let himself forget was Eric's sense of responsibility for Ben. After all, Eric had watched after Ben on those same streets for many nights and days.

Eric had proven he was thinking about what he was doing, though, as he had taken Pete's second cell phone, the one Pete used if it would be awkward for his calls to be traced back to him. Ben had no way to communicate where he was or if he needed help; Eric did, and Pete had no doubt that if Eric found Ben, he would call. Because, while Ben might not trust Pete, Eric did.

This confidence in Eric was something new, and it gave Pete a warm feeling. Pete also felt certain Eric would find Ben and would seek Pete's help as soon as he did. That knowledge was the only thing helping Pete hold on to his sanity.

# TWENTY-FIVE

Marge knew something was wrong as soon as she walked into the Dusty police station Saturday morning. She didn't know why Carl had called, asking her to come, and she didn't know why the county police officers were there. The electricity in the air warned her something had happened even before she saw Brent slumped in a chair in the holding cell.

"Why is Brent here?" she asked.

Brent looked up, his eyes bloodshot. As soon as he saw her, his face contorted in anger. "It's your fault," he said, his voice barely a whisper. "If you hadn't been poking around I wouldn't have had to move him."

Marge turned to Carl. "What's my fault?"

"Eugene Martell never woke up. The doctor thinks the sedative Brent gave him was too much for his system to handle in his weakened condition."

"Did you use the same sedative you did on Alfred and Jerry?" Marge asked.

"I didn't give *anyone* a sedative. Hugo gave my father one, to keep him calm during the move. I thought he knew what he was doing."

"Marge, that was over the top," Carl warned. "The man just lost his father."

Did they think it was her fault Eugene died, because

she had been nosing around? She ran a hand over her face. Wasn't it Brent's fault, for trying to hide his own actions by drugging his father? Still, Carl was right; she didn't need to be cruel.

"Yes, it was," she said. "I'm sorry." She looked around. "That still doesn't explain why Brent is here and not in the county jail. There is nothing he can do for his father now."

Carl looked uncomfortable. "Well, the county guys were wondering … since Brent might have felt threatened by you following him … and since his father died … well, if you might consider…"

He took one look at Marge's face and stopped.

"Not pressing charges?" she asked, her voice rising. "Not pressing charges for being manhandled, threatened with a gun, restrained, and listening to him instruct his henchman to get rid of me in a fiery crash?"

The county officer stood straighter. "We didn't know all that, ma'am," he said, shooting a look at Carl. "Did you tell anyone?"

Marge looked from one to the other. "At least wait until you have a chance to listen to the recording Pete made from my phone. In addition to Brent's plans to kill me, which he made perfectly clear, I believe it will raise doubts about Brent's innocence in Dan's murder and the attack on Leroy."

The county officer removed Brent from the holding cell. "All right, it's back to lockup for you," he said.

"Wait," Marge said. She turned to Brent. "Why did you do it? Did you move your father to prevent anyone from talking with him? What were you afraid he would tell us?"

"I wanted to move my father to a facility where his needs

would be better met than at home. I had him sedated to make the trip less traumatic for him. How could I know—?" Brent looked like he was about to break down with honest emotion. "How could I know the sedation would be too much for him?"

Marge steeled her heart against his obvious pain. "Did his doctor okay the sedation?"

"I don't have to answer any more of your questions."

"But why did you say it was my fault you had to move your dad when you just said you moved him because of his condition?" she pursued.

"I'm so upset, I hardly know what I'm saying," he replied. But the look he shot Marge told her he wasn't being so honest anymore.

"What have you done with Hugo?" Marge asked the county officer.

The officer shook his head. "He managed to elude us. We're still looking for him. By using your sketch we were able to identify him as Hugo Walsh and discovered there are several warrants out on him for assault and robbery."

"Any history of drugging his victims?" she asked.

"None that we found. But he did train with a pharmacy for a clerk's position several years ago. He was expelled after some drugs came up missing and he was suspected of stealing them."

"Clerk's position?" Brent exclaimed. His eyes opened wide before he clamped his mouth shut.

As the officer led Brent out of the Dusty police station to return him to the Pasco jail, Marge wondered why Brent was so shocked to hear Hugo had been a clerk. Suppose Brent hired Hugo to provide drugs Brent could use on

Alfred and Jerry. Did Brent also ask Hugo to sedate his father, believing Hugo knew more about drugs than he actually did? Was Eugene Martell dead because Hugo lied about his background?

Marge sank into a chair and rubbed her eyes. If she wasn't so tired, maybe she could think straight.

"Are you ready to go home now, Marge?" Carl asked.

Marge looked up, her shoulders sagging. "Why were you trying to get me to drop the charges against Brent? Don't you believe me?"

Carl looked down. "I believe you about what happened to you, Marge. I'm just not sure about the rest of it. And I'm afraid. What is going to happen to Dusty now? If Brent took over his dad's estate, he might continue his father's plans because he would be the power on the throne. With him gone, too, what future does this town have?"

Marge shook her head. "I wish I knew how to get at the truth, Carl. And yes, I do have to go home. My other foster son needs me. But I haven't accomplished what needed to be done here. I thought Eugene Martell could tell us what was behind the killing and attempted murders—but he didn't have a chance. Before I leave town, I want to have another talk with Eugene's attorney. You might want to do that, too."

"Why?"

"I told you, Eugene changed his power of attorney from Brent to Mr. Leonard only a few months ago. Maybe Mr. Leonard knows something he couldn't tell us while Eugene was alive. He indicated the change meant Eugene no longer trusted Brent to carry out his wishes. So, what other contingency plans might Eugene have made?"

Marge felt almost guilty for the look of hope that blossomed on Carl's face because she had a sick feeling that whatever plans Eugene was making, he hadn't had a chance to carry them out before Brent took control of his life.

Realizing she did not have her cell phone, Marge asked Carl if she could use an office phone to call Mr. Leonard. She also asked Carl where she could purchase a temporary track phone before they headed out of town.

When Marge picked up the receiver, she realized she did not know the attorney's number. Sensing her dilemma, Carl said, "I talked with Mr. Leonard yesterday." He pulled out his cell phone and read off the number to her.

Mr. Leonard was shocked to discover his client had died during the night and no one had informed him.

Marge explained the circumstances. "Brent is in the county jail for attacking me. And he might bear some culpability in his father's death, but many questions still remain unanswered about why and whether the other recent events in Dusty are connected. Carl Whiting is also concerned about the future of Dusty with both Eugene and Brent out of the picture. I have to return to Bellevue as soon as I can, but before I do, I wondered if Carl and I could have a word with you?"

The attorney agreed to meet with them in his office in Prosser, in case he needed to reference his records there.

~

An hour later, Carl and Marge arrived at Ron Leonard's office. Although Carl drove them in his car, they made a stop on the way for Marge to purchase a temporary cell phone.

Once they were settled in the attorney's office, Marge jumped right in. "I think you know I'm especially interested in Dan and Leroy, one murdered and the other attacked, who I have reason to believe are Eugene's biological sons. Carl is more interested in whether there is anything set up as far as continuing support for the development of Dusty."

"I have a little bit of a problem, because Eugene indicated he was changing his will, but he had not yet informed me of the changes he wished to make," Ron Leonard said. "Of course, unless he had any changes properly witnessed, they won't be considered. Still, it would be good to know what was on his mind.

"I'm not sure I should tell you this, but the secret seems to have caused so much trouble I'm going to go out on a limb. Please keep it quiet unless you need the information to make sure justice is done. Eugene supported both Dan and Leroy while they were growing up. He paid for their education, and continued to support their mothers after the boys were grown and on their own. As soon as he discovered he was terminally ill, he set up a trust to continue supporting the two women for the rest of their lives. However, these benefits would cease if the recipients ever revealed what they were receiving or why."

Marge's head spun. "So, the changes Eugene indicated he was going to make to his will probably do not include adding Dan and Leroy because they had already been provided for?"

"I've reviewed the last will I have on file for Eugene, and

in it he does make sizable provisions for Dan and Leroy, but not ongoing support. The bulk of the estate goes to Brent. However, since Eugene was unhappy with Brent's lifestyle, he might have been planning to change the ratio in some way, or even cut Brent out entirely."

"Or Brent might have been convinced Eugene was going to cut him out; so he kept his father under wraps to keep him from changing his will."

"My guess would be yes. I've talked with Eugene's physician, who indicates there was no reason to believe Eugene's condition would have affected his mental capacity. Brent evidently spread that rumor so no one would question his father being sequestered at the mansion."

"So, we are at a dead end," Marge said. "We can only guess how Eugene intended to change his will and whether Brent discovered it. I believe Brent killed Dan and intended to kill Leroy to ensure they would not be able to inherit from his father. I believe he set Alfred and Jerry up for the crimes. But, I have no way to prove any of this."

"Eugene made no provision for Dan and Leroy's shares to go to their heirs if they predeceased him; so their deaths would preserve the whole estate for Brent—unless of course, he was disinherited."

"So, what happens to the will with Brent in jail?"

"It depends on how the court interprets what happened. If the inheritance is not the result of a crime, Brent will receive it."

"And, if we find another will?"

"If we find a more recent, legally acceptable will, of course it would invalidate this one."

"What if we find some handwritten notes by Eugene

that state how he intended to change his will?" Marge knew the answer, but she was grasping at straws.

Mr. Leonard shook his head. "Unfortunately, that would not matter. In the state of Washington, even a handwritten will must have two witnesses for the signature to be valid."

"And Brent had Eugene under lock and key; so he couldn't get any witnesses." Marge heaved a sigh. Even if they found a document to prove what Eugene intended, it would do them no good now.

She looked at Carl. "Unfortunately, I guess that answers your question about continued support for Dusty, too."

"Not completely," Mr. Leonard interjected. "I don't know how much money Eugene has spent in Dusty, but his aim was always for the town to become self-supporting. The housing development is complete and the owners are paying property taxes. He bequeathed the café to the current managers, and it also pays taxes. The library, as well as the police and fire stations, are free of debt. He has already made arrangements to expand solar and wind-energy production, with contracts Brent would have difficulty breaking.

"In addition, Eugene made me administrator of another trust with the purpose of helping Dusty make the transition to a self-supporting town." He looked at Carl. "The first thing you will need to do is get the residents together to establish some type of town governance."

Tension Marge hadn't noticed before seeped out of Carl. "I was wondering if I would still have a job," he said.

"You—or someone—will probably get an upgrade to sheriff's deputy before this is over," the attorney said.

"How many trusts can you get out of one estate?"

Mr. Leonard laughed. "You can't even imagine how wealthy Eugene was. He was a wizard on the stock market, and in addition to large stock bonuses while he worked for Microsoft during its years of explosive growth, he was heavily invested in Del Monte and ConAgra for several of their best years. Brent had no reason to worry about his inheritance as long as he wasn't written out of the will entirely. He'll hardly be able to use a fraction of it, even with his lifestyle."

"It's too bad he didn't know that," Marge said. "Thank you for being open with us, Mr. Leonard. I still can't prove what I believe happened to Dan and Leroy, but at least I have a better understanding of what brought it about."

~

"So, you're heading to Bellevue today?" Carl asked as they approached Dusty.

"After I get my cell phone issue resolved. At the least, I'd like to transfer my information to this new phone. Of course, if the county police have questions for me ... well, I could always come back. Right now, I am needed at home. I hope something I've said convinces you to keep looking for Dan's killer. Don't let Alfred be railroaded."

"You don't believe there is any possibility he did it?"

Marge shook her head. "No. I don't. I wish there was a way I could prove it."

"I'll keep an open mind," Carl promised as he dropped her off at her car. "Have a safe trip home."

"Thank you. Say good-bye to Angela and Carla and

Joey for me, will you? I hope we can see you again, under better circumstances."

Marge stopped at the library to say good-bye to Cynthia and thank her for her assistance. Then she popped in at the Dusty Café to purchase a coffee and sandwich for the road.

On her way toward Route 17, she slowed in front of the Martell house. Eugene had put so much time and money into creating a modern wonder of a home and turn a bunch of abandoned, rundown buildings into what could soon be a model town. Too bad his weakness for women threatened everything he had accomplished.

On impulse, she swung in at the driveway. With no cars in sight, she drove past the front entry and, with a nervous glance behind her, drove the Honda around to the side of the house, out of view from the road. She had no intention of breaking in, but, as quickly as Hugo had left last night, she wondered ...

# TWENTY-SIX

～～～～～

Marge caught her breath. The back door was unlocked and the alarm system was deactivated. She hesitated before walking inside. Should she do this? No, of course not. Carl had told her what he would do if he caught her trespassing again. She should get back in her car and keep going to Pasco so she could go home.

Not listening to reason, she slipped through the door and closed it behind her, finding herself in the kitchen. All right, she was inside, but she wouldn't touch anything. Just a quick look around. She pulled paper towels off a roll beside the sink to cover her hands. No need to confuse anyone by accidentally putting her fingerprints where they didn't belong.

She looked around the kitchen and wrinkled her nose. Brent had obviously stopped any kind of housekeeping service, and Hugo hadn't bothered to clean up after himself. Food-encrusted plates and utensils filled the sink and counter space.

A cursory inspection showed no signs of any drugs. Would anyone hide drugs in the kitchen? She thought it might be too obvious to hide them among similar-looking items, and a little dangerous for the same reason. Anyway, they would hardly be in plain view and she didn't have time to search through the spices and staples in the pantry. If she didn't find any suspicious drugs in the house, she was out of luck because the chances of the outbuildings also being unlocked were slim, especially if they had incriminating evidence in them.

She didn't expect to find anything in the living or dining rooms, and she didn't; nor did she see any good hiding places. Books lined the walls of the only other room downstairs. Marge groaned. She didn't have time to pull books off the shelves to see if anything was hidden behind them. She'd look everywhere else before spending any time searching there.

Upstairs, she glanced into three well-appointed bedrooms, each with its own bathroom, sitting area, and slider to a deck that spanned the back and one side of the house. A quick check of the medicine cabinets turned up nothing suspicious. Again, a little too obvious.

The next room she found was an office. Rifling through the desk drawers, it quickly became clear this was Eugene's domain. No drugs were likely to be stashed here, but papers Eugene was working on for his will might be. While they might not be legal, they would show what he was planning and perhaps what Brent was trying to prevent.

Glancing out the window, she saw its view of the driveway and realized it was the same window where she had seen Eugene peering out. Fortunately, the driveway was still empty, because she needed time to see what Eugene might have left.

She found nothing more than bills, receipts, stock reports, and correspondence with various agencies in the drawers. Of course, anything Eugene wanted to hide from

Brent would have to be in a locked drawer or safe, and Marge didn't find one of those in the office. Nor did she locate a key for such a hiding place. Anyway, she was running out of time. She had to keep moving.

She let her mind work on possible hiding places for both the drugs and any documents Eugene might have been working on. She shook her head at the library door. In the same way the kitchen seemed too obvious for hiding drugs, she felt the library seemed too obvious for papers. He must have another hiding place.

Of course, a new will, legal or not, wouldn't help her prove Brent killed Dan. Her best hope was to find the sedative Hugo had given Eugene and figure out how to determine if Brent used it on Alfred and Jerry.

Retracing her steps to the kitchen, Marge wondered again what she thought she was doing inside the house. No matter how she tried to justify her presence, she knew she was trespassing. Still, she couldn't stop herself from peeking into drawers and cupboards as she made her way out. She stopped short when she spotted a ring of several keys hanging from the inside of a cupboard door.

There was not enough time for her to find out what all the keys went to, inside or out. She decided she would take the time to try to unlock a door in the nearest building, which appeared to be a tool shed.

Leaving the house, a chill crept down Marge's back. She glanced over both shoulders as she scurried to the tool shed. She was being silly; no one was around to be watching her.

She tried several keys on the door, growing frustrated. None of them worked. All of a sudden, the door burst open and rough hands grabbed her.

"Hugo! I thought you'd be long gone by now," she cried as he dragged her in and slammed the door, locking it and throwing a deadbolt high on the side.

"Had some stuff to do first. Besides, best place to hide is right under their noses." He squinted his steely eyes at her. "Since you so conveniently showed up here, maybe I should arrange that fiery car accident for you."

Hugo shoved her aside, holding up a key and grinning wickedly. "Is this what you were looking for?"

"Why kill me now? It won't do Brent any good and everyone will know it was you." Marge turned so Hugo could only see her left side as she slipped her right hand into her pocket. Going by feel, she found what she thought was the talk button on her new cell phone and tried to dial 911. Spotting a pile of tools, she bumped into them, hoping the clatter they made as they fell would cover the sound of the call.

Hugo grabbed her arm and twisted her around, pulling the phone out of her pocket and tossing it into a corner.

"Think I'm as stupid as that spoiled brat who hired me?"

"Why are you still here?" Marge asked. Her eyes widened as she looked around. This wasn't a tool shed. It was a sophisticated workshop. Evidently Eugene had been a builder and a tinkerer as well as an engineer. "Getting rid of the drugs you and Brent used on Dan, Leroy, and Eugene?"

"What drugs?" he snarled, even as Marge saw him drop a plastic bag of white powder into his pocket and peer around as if he was looking for something.

"Oh, come on. You can tell me. You're going to kill me anyway." There were a lot of tools in here. Her challenge was to keep Hugo distracted until she could grab one she could use.

"I'm not going to kill you, you dumb broad. I don't need a murder charge hanging over my head." Hugo reached over and pulled a skein of heavy twine off a shelf.

Marge's head jerked up. "So, it was Brent, not you, who shot Dan and ran Leroy off the road. Did he drug Alfred and Jerry, too, so they wouldn't remember what they were doing?"

Hugo shook his head. "You really think I'm gonna say something to turn him against me? With the money he's got to get himself out of trouble and me into it?" As he reached to grab Marge's arm, she stepped close to him and stomped on his foot.

"Ouch," he said, grinning as he succeeded in grabbing her arm. Before Marge could react, Hugo had spun her around and pinned her arms behind her back. "I see you got some of them self-defense moves, but I got steel-toed boots," he said as he pulled her over to a bench, sat her down, and secured her wrists behind a steel girder before wrapping more twine around her ankles.

Marge expected him to leave. He had what looked like the remains of the drug and she was effectively locked up. Instead, he began rummaging around. He evidently found what he was looking for, reached over one of the cabinets, grabbed another key he seemed to know would be there, and opened a thin metal box. He pulled out a sheaf of papers. After he had scanned them, he started to laugh.

"He killed those guys for nothing," he said.

"You found Eugene's new will!" Marge exclaimed.

"Yep. And it doesn't say anything about Dan and Leroy; so whatever's in his last will about them hasn't changed. But Brent was not so lucky."

"How did you know Eugene kept his papers here?"

"I saw him bring them to the tool shed and watched where he hid them, but I didn't look at them because I didn't care, and Brent didn't pay me to snitch. I never told Brent because I thought they might be my insurance policy. Turns out, they won't help me now. Well, I gotta go." Hugo threw the papers down at Marge's feet. "I'm not sticking around for that SOB to try and pin everything on me; so I don't need these. Sure hope someone finds you before it gets too hot."

"You'd leave me here to die? That's murder. You said you didn't do murder."

Hugo studied her for a long moment. "Nah, I kind of like you. You got spunk. I'll probably let somebody know you're here after I'm far enough away."

"No!" Marge cried to no avail.

Hugo closed and locked the door behind him. She jerked against the twine that bound her to the girder. "I have to get home."

She stared at the door. Panic brought a scream to her throat, but no sound came out. Closing her eyes, she took two deep breaths before she could stop shaking. She needed to be calm. She needed to think.

She had already found a rough spot on the girder. She began to methodically rub the twine up and down over it. The metal bit into her skin. Soon she felt a trickle of blood run down her hand. She gritted her teeth. She wouldn't let herself get distracted. She would rub that twine up and down until it split apart no matter long it took and no matter how many cuts she gave herself.

Because she had spunk.

She laughed as tears rolled down her cheeks and she rubbed at the twine.

# TWENTY-SEVEN

~~~~~~

Marge let out her breath in a small explosion when the twine suddenly gave. She worked to unravel the strands. The numbness in her fingers frustrated her. Finally, she removed the last thread and fumbled at the knots in the twine around her ankles. They refused to give. Thank goodness Hugo hadn't thought to anchor her legs on anything. She stood and took a tiny, wobbly hop towards a toolbox.

Not an easy endeavor. Her legs, bound together in an awkward position, didn't give her much balance. She wavered, arms out to steady herself, and caught hold of a post with her right hand. She held on as she tried another couple of hops, wincing at the pain shooting through her ankles. After what felt like an hour, she reached the tools.

She sent up a silent prayer of thanks when she found a box knife in the kit and managed to hobble to a place to sit nearby. She didn't know how much longer she could have stood with her legs tied together at such an awkward angle. Her fingers were still numb so it took longer than she expected to cut the twine, which frustrated Marge again. She let out an explosive sigh of relief when the last strands of twine finally gave without inflicting any additional damage to her ankles.

Hobbling to the door, she unlocked it and took deep gasps of the fresh air. She checked her wrists and decided she could put off first aid on the cuts and scratches for a while.

She waited until her head had cleared and she had better control of her legs before she returned to the workshop and scrounged in the corner where Hugo had thrown her cell phone. She called Pete first, to let him know she was all right and might be a little delayed but still hoped to get home tonight. She called Carl next, thankful she had memorized his number, and told him where she was. She didn't give either of them time to ask questions. She couldn't handle questions yet.

Gathering up the papers Hugo had scattered in front of her, she walked around to the front of the house to wait on the porch, unwilling to stay cooped up for another minute.

In less time than she would have imagined possible, Carl drove in, closely followed by a county patrol car.

"What did you think you were doing?" Carl demanded.

"I admit I was snooping where I didn't belong. I thought if I didn't do it, no one would, and we would never get to the truth."

"So, did you get to the truth?"

"Nothing you can use in court," she admitted, handing Carl the papers. "I haven't even read these, but Hugo told me they didn't mention Dan or Leroy."

"Hugo was here?" the county officer exclaimed. "How long ago did he leave?"

Marge frowned. Time had lost its meaning while she was working on her escape. "It must be a little over an hour," she guessed. "He refused to say anything to implicate

Brent, because he's afraid of the kind of justice Brent's money can buy, but he accidentally blurted out 'He killed those guys for nothing,' after he read these." She absent-mindedly rubbed her arms. Carl grabbed her wrists and inspected them.

"We need to get you to the hospital," he said.

Marge envisioned a long, agonizing wait in an emergency room. "No, I need to go home. A little antiseptic will do for now."

The county officer had gone to his car while Marge and Carl were talking. When he returned, he said, "I've let everyone know Hugo is still in the area. We'll need to take you in for questioning," he added, looking hard at Marge.

Marge felt tears well up again. "I can't tell you anything more than I already have," she said. "I'm sorry. I know I stepped over the line here, but I really, really have to get home. You can ask me anything you want to on the phone after I get there."

The look on the officer's face told Marge that wasn't going to happen.

She was surprised to hear Carl come to her defense. "Mrs. Peterson's husband is a homicide detective in Bellevue," he said. "She isn't going anywhere; and, if truly needed, she has already said she can come back for questioning. But she has a child at home who needs her now."

"She should have thought about her child before she decided to trespass on private property," the officer said.

"Yes, she should have," Carl agreed.

"Yes, I should have," Marge repeated. "I thought I might be able to resolve some issues by taking a look. Nothing was disturbed except in the workroom out back, and most of the disturbing out there was done by Hugo."

"I'm sorry. You might still be able to leave tonight, but it will be much later. You need to come in now and make a statement. We'll try to make it as quick as possible." The officer was not budging.

"Oh, well. Maybe I can get my cell phone back? Or if you still need it may I transfer the information to this new one? I was planning on stopping on my way home to ask."

"You can have your phone back. The recording your husband made is helpful and we have made a copy of it, but we have no way to trace it back to your phone; so there is nothing useful on your phone for us."

"You should be glad you're still alive," Carl said to Marge after the officer walked away to inspect the tool shed.

"Hugo said he's not a murderer—and I actually tend to believe him," Marge said. "I'm sure Brent did the killing, especially since Hugo said 'he killed them for nothing.' But I don't know how it can ever be proven." She lifted her chin into the air. "Hugo also said I have spunk."

Carl stared at her for a moment before bursting out with laughter. "Yes, Marge Peterson, whatever else you have, you definitely have spunk."

Marge frowned. "It has occurred to me that we don't necessarily have to prove Brent killed Dan—although I'd prefer it if we could. What we've found out, though, convinces me he did it, and it might throw too much doubt on the case against Alfred for him to be convicted."

Carl nodded. "Possible. That's out of my hands. However, I do have some good news for you."

"I could use some," she said.

"Leroy is awake and was able to talk to a detective. He says he got a glimpse of the driver of the car that pushed him off the road. It wasn't Jerry."

"He's positive?"

"Yes. He and Jerry played basketball together in high school. Jerry's looks might have been a bit ravaged by time and drink, but the driver of the other car didn't look anything like Jerry."

Marge held her breath. "Was it Brent?"

"Leroy says he can't be sure."

Marge let out a deep sigh. "So, Jerry is in the clear for sure. I hope Alfred will be released, for insufficient evidence. Even if he isn't, I can assure Eric without a doubt in my mind that his grandfather isn't a murderer. Unfortunately, even if we could prove beyond a shadow of a doubt Alfred didn't do it, there still might not be enough evidence to convict Brent."

"I still believe there is enough evidence against Alfred to hold him," Carl said. "After all, it was his gun, on his property, and he was so drunk he doesn't know what he was doing. Besides, who knew Dan was going to be there?"

Marge stared at Carl. That was a good question—and one she had not thought enough about. Who, besides Dan's mother and Carl, knew Dan was going to see Alfred? And how did that person find out?

And who knew Leroy was going to be driving on a country road hardly anyone ever used?

~

After the police finished their inspection of the tool shed and surrounded it with yellow tape, everyone headed to the police station in Pasco. Carl and Marge followed in their separate cars.

They cleared the security kiosk together. Walking along the fenced sidewalk, Marge wondered who had thought of this layout. Anyone who forced entry through security would have a lengthy walk in an open area before reaching any building within the law enforcement compound.

A police officer met Carl and Marge and ushered them past a beehive of activity: patrolmen leading people in handcuffs to their desks, others busy talking on their phones, and others studying their computer monitors. Their guide ushered them into an office with a window overseeing the sea of activity and indicated seats with their backs to it.

"This is Captain Wilkers," the officer said. He turned to the captain. "This is Marge Peterson, who has been heavily involved with the investigation and who lodged the complaint against Brent Martell. I believe you know Carl Whiting."

A commotion outside his office drew the captain's attention before they could sit down. Turning, Marge gasped. Hugo was being dragged in, his hands cuffed behind his back.

*How does that feel to you?* she couldn't help thinking.

"Well," Captain Wilkers said. "I guess our session will have to wait a bit while we see what this gentleman has to say for himself." He gave Marge a crooked grin. "I believe you have earned yourself a front row seat to the interrogation."

Hugo didn't seem to have lost any of his cockiness, even

though he sat handcuffed across the table from a police detective. The interrogation was short and uneventful. Hugo was familiar with the system and demanded to have an attorney before talking.

Back in his office, Captain Wilkers told Carl and Marge that Hugo didn't have an attorney of his own, so he would be assigned a public defender.

"I'm sure Brent already has an attorney; and probably a high-powered one," Marge said.

"Yes, he does," said the captain.

"If I were Brent, I'd hire an attorney for Hugo. In fact, I think Hugo expects him to. What better way to keep Hugo on his side and, with the attorneys working together, they could keep the police from playing one against the other. It might even help Brent if he decides to throw Hugo under the bus."

The men all stared at her.

"I mean, Hugo came this close to telling me straight out Brent drugged Alfred and Jerry, killed Dan, and ran Leroy off the road. I have a feeling the overdose on Brent's father truly was accidental. However, Hugo said he couldn't accuse Brent because he would be buried by the kind of legal talent Brent could buy. If Brent hired a good attorney for Hugo, he could make it certain Hugo won't talk.

"But I don't see how any lawyer, no matter how skilled, could put the blame on Hugo and leave Brent in the clear. What motive could Hugo possibly have? Anything he did would be on Brent's command."

"Marge …" Carl said, and Marge realized she had probably overstepped her bounds again.

"No, no, she's right. That's good thinking," Captain

Wilkers said, leaning back in his chair and tenting his hands over his chest. "However, if we make Hugo believe Brent is trying to put the blame on him, Hugo would have no incentive to protect Brent. It could work. But it will take a bit of finesse since we already have attorneys involved. As Mrs. Peterson predicted, Brent hired one for Hugo, also."

Marge cringed, anxiety overriding any satisfaction she might have felt at being right. Did finesse mean time? Had she opened her mouth and ruined any chance of going home today? She had to get home.

"Once both attorneys are here, we will put them in separate interview rooms with Hugo and Brent and frame our questions in such a way to lead both Brent and Hugo to believe they are being set up by the other to take the blame. In the meantime, Mrs. Peterson, let's go over everything you have been doing this past week."

Marge found herself liking this police captain and hoped Carl would be open to learning from him. After an hour of careful questioning, she was sure Captain Wilkers had elicited every move she had made and every bit of knowledge she had learned since she arrived in the area with Eric.

An officer poked his head in the door. "Showtime," he said.

~

Captain Wilkers started with Brent while Marge and Carl watched through the observation window. "We have an eyewitness who says the driver of the car that rammed into Leroy was you."

"What eyewitness?" Brent demanded, leaning forward. His attorney raised a warning hand and Brent sat back, frowning.

"Who else would want to kill Leroy?" asked the captain.

"You already got the guys who killed Dan and ran Leroy off the road. Do you have the maniac who killed my father, too?"

"Maniac? You mean Hugo, the man you hired to keep your father locked up in his own home?"

"What are you talking about? Hugo was my father's caretaker, not his guard. Why would I need to lock my father up? He was a sick old man."

"You wanted to be sure your dad couldn't change his will to benefit his other children."

Brent's eyes grew hard. "What other children? I am my father's only child."

"Not true," Captain Wilkers said, relaxing back in his chair and tenting his fingers over his chest again.

Marge thought he must make that gesture so often because it made him look as if he had a secret font of knowledge.

"Your father's attorney says Dan and Leroy are indeed your father's biological sons."

"That old phony! He's been playing my father for years. Now, what are you doing about the fake pharmacist who killed my father?"

"Fake pharmacist? Did Hugo tell you he was a pharmacist? I thought you said he was a 'caretaker.' Exactly how did he kill your father?"

"Hugo told me he knew what he was doing, but he gave my father an overdose of that sedative."

"The same sedative you used to knock out Alfred and Jerry Landon?"

Brent looked confused for a moment. "How ...?" He closed his mouth and glanced at his attorney. "What makes you think they were drugged? They drank enough to knock themselves out without any help from me."

"Some drugs can remain in the system for a long time—in the hair follicles. What do you suppose we'll find when we finish testing Alfred and Jerry?"

"How would I know?"

~

Behind the observation window, Marge shook her head and turned to Carl. "Unless either Hugo gives him up or Leroy remembers for sure it was Brent in the car, it doesn't sound to me as if there is enough to hold Brent for murder."

"So, it's a good thing we have his attack on you to keep him under lock and key for a while," Carl said.

"They are completely sober now; do you think there is any chance Alfred or Jerry might remember what happened in the few minutes before they blacked out?"

"Probably not. The captain is going to interview Hugo now. Let's see if he gets any further with him."

~

"Brent says you killed his father," Captain Wilkers began.

Hugo looked bored. "It was an accident," he said.

"But you gave him the sedative?"

"I only ever did what Brent told me to do."

"Brent says you claimed you knew what you were doing. He called you a 'fake pharmacist.'"

"I never claimed to be no pharmacist. I dropped out of school and worked in a drugstore."

"As a clerk."

"I never claimed to be no pharmacist," Hugo repeated.

"You got the sedative for him, though."

"I only ever did what Brent told me to do."

Hugo was beginning to sound like a broken record.

"So, did Brent tell you to drug Alfred and Jerry Landon?"

"I didn't drug them. Never saw them. Don't even know what they look like."

"But you got the drug for Brent?"

"I only ever did …"

"All right, all right," Captain Wilkers said. "I don't suppose you have an alibi for the time Dan was killed or Leroy was attacked."

"I was at the Martell place, with the old man. Never left him alone."

"So there is no one who can back you up?"

"Only Brent."

"Brent was with you the whole time, both times?"

For the first time, Marge saw a flicker of doubt in Hugo's eyes. He glanced at his attorney, as if looking for guidance. "Didn't say that," he mumbled. He looked up. "If I'd a left the old man alone, he might have run out. What?" he added at a quick jab from his attorney.

"So, you were guarding Eugene."

"He wandered," Hugo said, his jaw jutting out defensively. "Had to protect him."

"But his doctor said there was nothing wrong with his mind. If he wandered, it was because he wanted to get out from under your control."

Hugo's expression closed down. "I only ever did what Brent told me to do."

~

Marge shifted in her chair until the captain finished questioning Hugo and came out of the interview room.

"May I leave now?" she asked.

"Yes, I'm sorry. I thought you would want to hear what those two had to say for themselves. I know you need to head home."

"I did. Thank you for allowing me to observe. And, yes, I do need to head home. But I have two questions I want answered before I depart. And, you said that you were finished with my cell phone?"

"Yes, you can take it with you," the captain said, gesturing to an officer to retrieve it for her. "Thank you for all of your help with this investigation."

Marge gave him a quick look. He seemed to be sincere. What a surprise.

# TWENTY-EIGHT

Time was getting away from her, but Marge was determined to wind things up before heading for home. Her first stop was the hospital. She pulled her sketchbook out of her luggage and turned to the page with the drawing she had done of Brent at the Dusty Café. It was as good a likeness as she could do, even after seeing him at closer range today.

Tucking the sketchpad under her arm, she ran to the entrance. Once inside, she managed to slow to a fast walk until she was in front of Leroy's room.

"What do you want now?" Leroy's mother demanded, taking a stance as if to bar Marge from entering.

"May I see Leroy for a moment? I'd like to clarify something that might prove who ran him off the road."

Leroy's mother hesitated a moment, eyeing her warily. With a weary sigh, she stepped aside, waved Marge into the room, and followed.

"Hi. I'm so glad to see you are recovering, Leroy," Marge said. "I'm Marge Peterson, from Bellevue. I've been assisting the police with your accident. I was hoping you could help clear up some things. You told the police you couldn't be sure if Brent was driving the car that ran you off the road. Is it because you didn't get a good look at the driver?"

"No, the face I saw in the car is etched in my memory forever," said Leroy. "I didn't get a chance to tell the police why I wasn't sure if it was Brent or not. I was a couple of years behind Brent in high school, so I don't have a good recollection of what he looked like as a teenager, let alone what he would look like now; so I couldn't tell if it was him."

"So," Marge said, turning her sketchpad so Leroy could see her drawing, "is this the man who was driving the car?"

"Yes," Leroy said. "That's the face I saw. Is that Brent?"

"It is. I'm not sure I should have shown this to you, and I hope I haven't contaminated your testimony in any way." She turned to Leroy's mother. "Could you get in touch with the police and ask them to bring a recent photo of Brent to prove Leroy can identify him?"

Leroy's mother agreed, tears in her eyes. "Yes, but why don't you handle it yourself?" she asked.

"I have one more issue to solve here before I can go home to my family and my own problems," Marge said. "I don't suppose anyone told you Dan planned to visit Alfred?"

"No," she said, shaking her head. "I didn't even know about Dan. Why would anyone contact me?"

"No reason at all," Marge said. "I'm just trying to think of all the possibilities, to see which ones I can rule out in order to get to the truth."

~

Back in her car, Marge drummed her fingers on the steering wheel. Finally, she pulled out her cell phone and found the number for Ron Leonard.

"Mrs. Peterson, I thought you'd be halfway to Bellevue by now," the attorney said.

"I'd like to be," Marge replied. "But there is one key piece to this puzzle I need to find before I can go. I need to get in touch with Dan's mother, but I don't know how to reach her. And even if I knew how to contact her, I know she won't give me the information I need because she is sworn to secrecy about who Dan's biological father is."

"What do you want to know?"

"I need to know if she or Dan told anyone he was going to visit Alfred the day he was killed."

"I can ask her, if you don't think she'll respond to you."

Marge sat in the car, hoping the attorney could get in touch with Dan's mother right away, and she wondered what she would do with the information.

Marge was sure Dan's mother had told someone. There was no other way word could reach the killer in time for him to set up the elaborate plan to kill Dan and put the blame on Alfred.

She couldn't figure out why anyone would tell Brent, but Dan's mother might have told Eugene, to warn him in case the visit started a domino effect of information getting out. Marge needed to discover how Brent might have learned about Dan's plan to visit Alfred.

~

A few minutes later, her phone rang. It was Mr. Leonard.

"Dan's mother called Eugene the day before Dan went to Dusty to visit Alfred. She told him Dan planned to apologize to Alfred for all the suspicion and accusations he had dealt with over the years. Eugene told her not to worry about it."

End of the line, Marge thought. Eugene knew what Dan planned to do, but he was dead; so she had no way to know if he had told anyone else.

"Is she positive she was talking to Eugene?" Marge asked. She knew she sounded desperate, but Brent practically had Eugene a prisoner in his own home. Anything was possible.

"I don't believe Eugene ever told Brent or anyone else he was the father of those two boys. Brent could have found out some other way, but we have no way to know whether he did; nor any way to know for sure who was on the phone with Dan's mother."

After disconnecting, Marge sat lost in thought for a few minutes. She was sure the only way they would get more information was if Hugo turned against Brent. Unfortunately, she couldn't wait around for him to do it. She had more pressing concerns at home.

She dialed Carl's number. "How are things going over there?"

"We're sort of at a stalemate. While Brent won't say anything except how Hugo killed his father, Hugo won't roll over on Brent, either."

"Well, I think we have Brent for the attack on Leroy. Turned out Leroy wasn't sure it was Brent because he hadn't seen Brent since high school. I showed him a sketch of Brent and he recognized it right away as the man in Jerry's car. I asked Leroy's mother to have the authorities take a recent photo of Brent to show Leroy so there can be no doubt."

"So, we've got Brent for attempted murder and possibly Hugo for manslaughter."

"Yes, and we might have reasonable doubt about Alfred killing Dan, but I'd feel better if we could prove he was innocent. The day before Dan was killed, his mother spoke on the phone to someone she thought was Eugene about Dan going to visit Alfred. I don't know how to prove Brent was the one she actually spoke to unless Hugo turned against Brent and said so. I hope he does, but I don't have time to wait and see. I really do have to head home tonight."

"I'll follow up with the information you have given us and see if we can make a dent with either Brent or Hugo. Have a safe trip home, Marge. It has been a challenge and a pleasure getting to know you and Eric. I hope you and your husband will remember you have family in Dusty, after you adopt Eric."

"Count on it," Marge said.

She laid her head back against the headrest for a moment. It was hard to leave without all the ends tied up in a neat bundle, but she had probably done as much as she could here. Now it was time to go home and take care of Benjamin.

# TWENTY-NINE

~~~~~~~~~~

Marge called Pete to let him know she was leaving Pasco. He told her Benjamin hadn't come home at all last night, and Eric was out looking for him.

She had to take several deep breaths before trusting herself to drive. It took constant vigilance to keep her speed under control.

Realizing she had been driving in a fog, she stopped in Ellensburg for coffee. She had no idea how fast she had been going or how she had arrived there, her mind had been busy bouncing around between the possibility of Alfred being wrongly convicted of murder and Benjamin somewhere in the dark streets of Seattle with his drugged out mother.

She was glad she had stopped for the refresher. A persistent drizzle began as she approached the top of Snoqualmie Pass. She knew the rain would make the road slick. She knew she should slow down, but the traffic swerving past her and hurtling around the mountain curves made going slower feel riskier than driving fast.

She breathed a sigh of relief when she turned onto I-405 for the final, traffic-clogged stretch home. Perhaps it was too soon to relax. The drizzle had turned into a steady downpour. The cars zooming past seemed oblivious to the decreased visibility. Her neck and shoulders ached as she concentrated on the road ahead of her and the traffic around her. Had she really wished for rain when she was in Pasco?

With a deep sigh of gratitude she exited the highway and maneuvered the side streets to her comfortable home. Marge pulled into the driveway and sat a few minutes, breathing deeply to alleviate the tension, before she dashed to the back door, leaving her suitcase in the car. She opened the door quietly, engulfed by the aroma of frying hamburger and onions and spied Detective Pete Peterson, her total hunk of a man, standing at the stove in one of her frilly aprons.

"Hey," she said.

Pete whirled around. "Hey, yourself." He turned the burner off and gathered Marge into his arms.

Marge basked in the comfort of those arms for a moment before looking around, hoping to see what she knew wasn't there. "What's the latest about Benjamin?"

"No word. Eric insisted he knows the streets and he knows Ben; so he had to go out there to find him. Of course, I didn't agree for Eric to go, but, as I told you, he left last night. No question, that's where he is."

Marge was deflated. "So, now we have both boys out on the street?"

Pete nodded. "And neither of us has a good understanding of where they lived or what neighborhoods they frequented in Seattle; so we have no way to find them. Since both boys are now missing, not just Ben's mother, the police are more involved in the search."

"They'll come back to us," Marge whispered. "I know

they will. I hope they won't have to suffer too much before they do." She looked at the stove. "So, who are you cooking for?"

Pete gave her the lopsided grin that always made her heart flutter. "You and the boys. They'll need some good home cooking when they return. And spaghetti with meat sauce is one of their favorites. Of course, in the refrigerator, I already have macaroni and cheese, and the makings for sloppy joes and pizza."

"So, you kept yourself busy cooking all the boys' favorite foods."

"Did a little shopping, too. In the liquor cabinet you'll find a variety of fine Columbia Crest red and Hogue Cellars white wines."

Marge laughed, but ended with a hiccup. "So, what do we do? Do we have to sit here and wait?"

Pete nodded. "It's all we can do, Marge. We have no hope of finding them ourselves, and everyone who does have some knowledge of the streets is looking, in Bellevue and in Seattle. Truth be told, Eric has a better chance than all of them combined."

"And we don't know anyone from their old life who can help us," Marge muttered. She frowned. "I wonder how much Jerry knew about Eric's life when he wasn't at home."

Pete snorted. "Jerry was drunk out of his mind most of the time. I doubt he even knew Eric wasn't home. Besides, it isn't where Eric would go. It is where Ben or his mother would go."

"Does Olivia have any ideas?"

"She had some, but none of them panned out."

"Who is looking for the boys?"

"Narcotics; Bellevue, King County, and Seattle. The night patrol that knows the most about prostitution. And every policeman who is out on the streets."

Tears formed in Marge's eyes. "I have often worried that the police weren't doing all they could on a case. It sounds as if this time they are."

Pete gathered her into his arms again. "They are, Marge. It doesn't make waiting any easier, but they are."

"When Eric returns, I'm buying him a cell phone," Marge said.

Pete stood back. "Where did that come from?" he asked.

"If he'd had a cell phone when he was in Dusty, he could have let me know where he was. And now, he could let us know if he had found Ben and his mother. Eric has learned responsibility the hard way, and I think we could trust him with a cell phone."

"Well, let's hope he has, because I forgot to tell you, Eric did take my secondary cell phone with him."

"Oh, thank God! Pete, I feel so helpless. I need to ask for God's help in handling this. I don't think we can do it alone."

Pete took her hand and led her to the living room, where they sat and bowed their heads in silent prayer. Marge couldn't even put into words the anxiety she was feeling. She could only lift up her hands to God and ask for His presence with Benjamin and Eric.

Her cell phone rang.

"Aunt Marge?" Eric's voice was small, shaking.

"Yes, Eric—Where are you?"

"Where are you?"

"I'm home. Where are you?"

"I found them. But it is awful. I don't know what to do.""

Marge's stomach clenched. "Benjamin …"

"Benji's mostly okay, but his mother … isn't. Can you …?"

"If you can tell me where you are, Eric, I'll have EMTs there as quickly as possible, and Pete and I will be right behind them."

"Yeah," Eric breathed, his voice steadier. He told Marge the address where he had found Benjamin and his mother.

"It's way creepy here. Hurry, please."

After making the call to 911, Pete and Marge jumped into Marge's Honda and sped off to the address Eric had provided. By the time they arrived, not only an ambulance but also a couple Seattle police cars were at the scene. It was a shady part of the city.

Pete flashed his badge to get the two of them inside, where Eric was huddled with a blood-covered Benjamin in a corner. Benjamin's mother was in the center of the activity, obviously dead, battered, and bruised.

Marge felt her stomach turn over. She wanted to grab Benjamin and remove him from this horrible scene. With effort, she made herself proceed cautiously. Who knew what was going on in Benjamin's mind after witnessing his mother's violent death? Or how he would react to Marge?

Arms clenched around his stomach, he looked up, his dazed eyes wide with pain. "I was supposed to protect her." His voice was a strangled whisper. "I didn't."

Marge started to reach out but saw him pull back from contact. "Benjamin, I know you wanted to protect your mother," she said, wrapping her arms around her stomach to control them from shaking. "But understand this:

it is the parent's responsibility to protect her child, not the other way around."

"She did." Benjamin broke down and sobbed. "She did protect me. That man wanted to get at me, and she wouldn't let him. He wouldn't have beat her and stabbed her if she would have let him have me. It's my fault."

Marge thought her heart would break. "No, son, it is not your fault. It is the fault of the man who did this horrible thing. But you can be proud forever that your mother gave her life to save you." She wasn't at all sure Benjamin took any comfort from her words, but he suddenly loosened up and collapsed in her arms in tears.

Eric watched from the corner where the two had been. She reached out her other arm and pulled him in. "Thank you, Eric. You did a very good thing today," she said.

A police detective walked over to them.

"I'm going to need statements from both of these boys," he said in a stern voice.

Pete stepped forward. "Of course you are," he said. "But Ben is pretty traumatized after seeing his mother beaten to death and Eric has been out on the streets for over twenty-four hours looking for them. I think it would be better if we took them home to clean up, pull themselves together, and get some rest before any questioning."

The detective looked reluctant, but finally agreed after Pete identified himself and promised to have the boys at the Seattle Police Department early the next morning.

"Don't forget you are an officer of the law," he said. "Don't allow these boys to concoct any stories."

"They don't need to concoct any stories," Pete stated in a voice that brooked no argument. "The truth is bad enough."

~

When they were home, Marge called Robert, Olivia, and Pete's mother to let them know everyone was safe. After the boys showered, Marge bagged their bloody clothes in case the police needed them, and she cleaned up the mess in the bathroom to minimize reminders in the morning.

Pete made hot chocolate and turned on the gas fireplace and they all sat in silence in the living room for half an hour, soaking up the comfort of being together. Marge wasn't about to tell the boys they had to go to bed.

"I'm hungry," Eric finally said. "There's some awful good smells in the kitchen."

Marge grinned. She had been waiting for that announcement. The resiliency of youth was wonderful, but she didn't think it would be quite so easy for Benjamin.

Pete motioned for Marge to stay with the boys and went into the kitchen, where Marge saw him throw out the hamburger he had been frying for spaghetti sauce. She guessed he was right. It had been sitting out for quite a while. A few minutes later, he returned with a platter of sloppy joes, paper plates, and napkins.

"We gonna eat in the living room?" Eric asked, his eyes wide with surprise. This was normally forbidden, especially while eating something with so much potential to cause stains.

"Just tonight," Marge said, nodding her head toward a still deflated Benjamin.

Eric caught her drift and nodded back before grabbing a sloppy joe.

"But be careful," Marge warned, handing him a plate to catch any drips.

Marge and Pete picked up their own sandwiches and began to eat, hoping Benjamin, who must be starving, would pick up one, too. They were halfway through theirs before his hand reached out. Once he had taken one bite, he ate ravenously and reached for a second one.

Marge felt tension ease from her body. It would be a long process, but the first step in healing had begun.

The ringing of Marge's cell phone jarred them. Marge answered, ready to hang up on whoever it was. Carl's voice stopped her.

"I know it's late, Marge, but I thought you would want to know what is going on here."

"Yes, I do," she said. Eric stopped eating and stared at her, either recognizing or guessing who was on the phone.

"You were right. Eventually Brent found a way to try to place the blame on Hugo. He claimed Hugo gave him opened bourbon bottles to take to Alfred and to Jerry, and that Hugo must have put some of the sedative in the bourbon. Hugo is still stonewalling, so we won't know what the drug was until we can get the powder we found on him tested."

"But why would Brent go to visit Alfred and Jerry?"

"Brent said he was trying to reach out to all the people in town since his father was dying, to assure them he would carry out his father's wishes."

"That's … bogus," Marge said, realizing how close she had come to saying something she wouldn't want the boys to hear her say. "He stopped progress on everything he could legally do before anyone realized he didn't have power of attorney for his father's affairs. Still, even if we give credence to this, what did he say Hugo's motive was?"

"Brent said he thinks Hugo decided that after Brent inherited everything, with so much money at his disposal, Brent might succumb to a little blackmail."

"Does Hugo still insist he 'only ever did' what Brent told him to do?"

"Exactly. Except now he is admitting that Brent told him to put the drug in the bottles."

Marge was sure enough of Carl's answer to her next question to put her phone on speaker. "So, does this prove Alfred did not shoot Dan?"

"It appears that it does. We expect to get Alfred out of prison tomorrow. Jerry is already released."

Eric smiled, but a worried look clouded his eyes. After disconnecting, Marge waited to hear what was on his mind. "I'm glad neither one of them is a killer," Eric said, "but does that mean one of them will get custody of me?"

"Don't borrow trouble," Pete said. "It takes time for these things to happen, and both your father and grand-father have a long history of not being able to stay sober."

Marge's phone rang again.

"Marge, this is Olivia. Jerry Landon called me a few minutes ago. He is back in Bellevue."

Marge stiffened. "What did he want?"

"While he is still sober and thinking straight, he wanted to let me know that he thinks you and Pete adopting Eric is the best thing for Eric. He just wanted to assure me that he and Alfred don't plan on putting up a fight—and they will both sign papers stating they will not interfere with you adopting him. He hopes you will not totally cut off contact with him and Alfred."

"As long as they are sober, that will be no problem," Marge said.

"Are we going to have any trouble adopting the boys because of all the things that have happened?"

"There will be some questions, but I'm confident we can answer them well enough to move ahead with the adoption proceedings."

"Thank the Lord, this is behind us," Marge murmured as she disconnected the call.

She looked over to see Benjamin asleep, leaning against Pete. Eric leaned on Pete's other side, fighting to keep his eyes open. Her heart warmed. With luck, they would soon be a legal family. She knew she was not going to get involved in any more crimes. She was going to stay right here and take care of her boys.

Unless, of course, something or someone threatened one of them.

# ACKNOWLEDGMENTS

Thank you to my writer's group in Traverse City: Tom Bonhort, Kathy Engstrom, Evelyn Harper, Leslie Lee, and Dzidra Minka, who gave valuable input into *When Will the Secrets End?*

Thanks as always to Mary Jo Zazueta, who gives honest and careful editorial feedback and makes the rest of the publishing process easy for me.

# ABOUT THE AUTHOR

PATRICIA K. BATTA, a Michigan native, attended Northwestern Michigan Community College in Traverse City, received her B.A. from the University of Puerto Rico, and finished at Oberlin College in Ohio with a Master's Degree in teaching.

Batta has been writing since she was ten years old, but began publishing after an early retirement. *When Will the Secrets End?* is the sixth book in the Marge Christensen Mystery series.

Batta has lived in Pennsylvania and Washington state. After being widowed, she returned to Michigan for ten years and now resides in Prescott, Arizona.

When not busy writing, she stays active with extended family, her church, and long road trips.

You may contact her via www.lillimarpublishing.com or www.patriciabatta.blogspot.com.